TROUBLE AT CAMP STILL WATERS

EDDIE GENEROUS

SEVERED PRESS
HOBART TASMANIA

TROUBLE AT CAMP STILL WATERS

ISBN: 978-1-925840-91-9

PROLOGUE

The cling and clang was on the air nearly as thick and steady as the deep-fryer scent. Six patrons remained in the diner after the supper crowd had departed, all men. The death toll explained on the TV hanging in the corner hadn't been entirely women, but a local serial killer had women more tentative than men.

Thirty-nine dead. Thirty-nine different modus operandi used. No clues. A million theories. For lack of a more promising course, law enforcement agreed that it *had* to be one killer.

It only made things worse that a group of nine teens had also gone missing. One girl had told her mother they were going camping in the woods, somewhere northwest, and not a trace of them had been seen since.

One killer, or ten killers, or thirty-nine killers, citizens were scared.

But money is money and while some had the luxury of hiding out, KC Brennan did not. Kraft Dinner didn't buy itself and fear didn't pay for new shoes or school supplies.

"Check?" she asked.

The man standing opposite the counter was big. Lumberjack big. He wore a heavy sweater with the right sleeve rolled above a cast on his wrist and forearm. He had a pleasant face, cool green eyes, light brown hair, and ears that stuck out like wings. A scar ran from his lower lip up to his cheekbone. Something nasty caused that one and there was some healing left to do yet. It was pink and shiny like a Barbie Doll's lipstick.

"Yes, please. Real nice smile you got there," the man said.

KC laughed, not at the forwardness, or clichéd sentiment of the comment, but at how it rang off a memory. In a life before children, KC had Hollywood dreams, at very least, of trying out for parts when Hollywood visited Vancouver—as it often did. First, the college for dramatic arts, be spotted from there, let an exec mold her, and then become a star. Famous actors gave interviews on TV and radio. KC mooned over these, picked and plucked, raking for nuggets and tips: watch movies, visit live theater, practice your craft. Practicing was free. Watching movies was cheap. Someday she'd have the cash for live shows, surely.

Not a day passed where KC didn't practice her screams, her fury, her tears. She practiced for her future before her mirror. And when she grew tired of that, she watched movies. Her mother had a Columbia House addiction that the company had no qualms about feeding. KC and her mother sat like junkies under the glow of the tube TV in the living room. Love stories, comedies, mysteries, dramas, science fiction, and horror, all of it. Horror was KC's favorite, especially the ones done well with strong humanity oozing off the screen like a toxic haze.

"You ever see that movie, *Henry: Portrait of a Serial Killer?*"

KC asked this man.

The man stiffened, slapped the cast on his wrist against his leg, and shined wide eyes on KC. It was momentary, two seconds, but it was something.

"Uh, no, darlin'," he said, unable to drop the gag he'd set out to play. *Henry* was his favorite movie and the first pillar of inspiration for his grand work. "No, I don't watch stuff 'bout killers. Enough of those out and about, don't ya think?"

KC looked at the cast. KC looked up the man's chest. KC's eyes met his. She flashed her smile, giving the best performance of her life.

"Killers or not, you ought to, it's a gem," she said and spun to ready the bill, half-certain this lug of a man was about to leap over the counter and end her days. Because, because, because, *it's him!*

The man had a ten in hand when KC brought her eyes back around. She handed off the slip.

The man read it. "Give me two bucks in quarters; need to do some laundry."

"Sure thing," KC said, already digging into her apron for change.

The man left and KC called a friend who lived in the apartment building behind the diner. It wasn't enough to call the police over, a hunch really. They likely had fifty bogus calls a day, but she had a *feeling*.

Trailing an Aerostar, Whitney Ruppert, wheeled her rust-bucket Camry a safe distance behind. She followed the man home. She staked out his crummy bungalow until two in the morning and then snuck off to KC's place. It was too much fun, but, like KC, Whitney had money to make.

At eight in the morning—KC's day off—she took Whitney's rust-bucket, loaded the boys, Willy and Timmy, into the backseat, and staked out the home. There was no movement all morning and the boys bitched incessantly. They went through seven dollars' worth of batteries, the Game Boys sucking the juice like WWF wrestlers and MLB all-stars.

Finally, at one in the afternoon, the Aerostar rolled. KC trailed it to a Zellers lot. The man got out, parking a good distance from the doors.

The light dimmed and finally, at seven, the man exited. KC and the boys followed him again. Across the city and to the university section. He parked in a shadowy lot outside a girls' dormitory. The van idled while the man hopped out. The side door slid open and the middle seat dropped onto the asphalt. Head down, the man scurried back to the driver's seat and rolled ten feet away. He parked, killed the engine, and approached the discarded seat.

It was only thirty seconds before the bus stopped on the street. Three young women exited, one approached the dorm. She wore the gawky uniform of a McDonald's employee.

The man picked up the heavy seat and began struggling it across the lot.

"Mom!" Timmy shouted from the backseat.

KC turned and glared. "You got to shut the fuck up now. If you both just shut the fuck up right now, I'll buy you new games. But you got to shut the fuck up." Her head shifted back to the window. The man hadn't heard the kid. He continued his work, grunting and groaning.

The reporters on the news had theories like everyone else did. KC agreed with Saša Petricic on the CBC that this monster appeared to be the *ultimate copycat killer*. The man dipped from nearly every famous serial murderer pool, and apparently dialogue from serial killer films too, and was now onto a Ted Bundy scheme.

The man fell forward over the seat, swore twice, and then rose, whining while wiggling the fingers of his right hand. The cast on his wrist reflected the light like an earthbound moon.

"Do you need some help?" the Micky D's scholar asked.

"No, go inside. Go inside," KC said.

"Oh geez, that'd be great," the man said.

As if scripted from start to finish. The seat re-entered the van via the side door and the man bashed the student over the head with three lightning strikes.

"Mom, can we go home yet?" Billy asked.

"Soon, soon."

KC kept a distance, terrified that her hunch paid too-real dividends and terrified for that poor woman in the van that she followed back to the bungalow. This time, once the man went inside with the woman draped over his shoulder, KC didn't stick around. She drove to the Bell telephone booth on the corner and had the operator put her through to the police.

The cops had heard enough from junior detectives. The cops were busy on a donut run. The cops had schedules loaded with profiling the Natives. The cops were in the middle of naps, taking sips of whiskey, tooting snorts of blow, whatever they were up to, they didn't give a damn about tips.

"Piss on you!" KC slammed the receiver and drove back to

the house. She parked and looked in the mirror at the boys. "Stay put for a minute. Mommy's gotta go take care of something."

The boys cried, sensing the danger.

On shaky legs, KC crossed the street, unsure of how to proceed. There was the van. There was the house. From within, the *Top Gun* theme song banged.

She was next to the van when the side door of the home opened. She dropped flat and tried to slide under the rusty frame. Not enough space. Footfalls swished toward her. She scampered up to her feet and broke for the back doors. Once there, she leaned against the bumper, shoulder pressed to the spare tire.

The sliding door announced its journey along the tracks. KC dropped to her butt when the van's interior light shined around her head like an angelic aura.

The man worked at some heavy labor inside the Aerostar. It shook and rocked on creaky shocks. The man grunted. Steel clanged on steel.

"Mom?" Billy shouted from the middle of the street.

KC turned her attention. Saw the boy under the orange streetlight glow. The man in the van had ceased moving.

"What are you doing, Mom?" Timmy asked, surging past his brother, running toward his mother.

KC's eyes widened and her mouth moved, gulping silently like a landed trout.

The man exited the van and stepped around the back, his pants clanged with rattling change. He hadn't gotten around to doing that laundry yet.

"Who you looking for, boys?" the man asked, passing KC.

"Mommy?" Billy said, fear slowing his pace.

Timmy had stopped. Billy stopped as soon as he joined his brother.

"Who's your mommy?" the man asked.

The boys held hands, staring at their mother, wishing her to her feet, wishing her to become the buffer zone of safety she'd always been.

The man turned around then and saw KC.

"Pretty smile. Say, you ever heard of Albert Fish? Ain't done my Albert Fish yet."

KC shot to her feet and the man smashed her face with the plaster cast on his wrist, swung in a clothesline whip. Her toes reached four feet high as her head rocked back. Blood spurted and flowed.

Timmy charged forward, latched onto the man's leg and bit down.

"Ow, you little shit!"

The man swung and conked a half-shot off the boy's head—no need to bruise the meat.

Billy stood in the street. Frozen until the man scooped him up. KC was a groggy mess when the man lifted her. At the front of the van, carting his trio—the boy's against his right hip, the waitress over his left shoulder—he first heard the sirens.

It was his turn to freeze as he listened.

Having to walk back from work had driven Whitney furious. When KC wasn't home, worry replaced anger. She called the police and got as far as KC had. It was only a block and decided to make a stink. Two hours after arriving, a young, skinny man, absolutely swimming in his uniform, took her complaint and decided to play hero, just in case.

He and another officer, one recently demoted to motor pool attendant, took Car-13 and rolled to Maple Street. Sirens blaring, two idiots stumbled onto the criminal that had plagued the province and garnered international attention. The hulking man side-eyed the street over his shoulder. When the cruiser broke hard at the end of his driveway, the killer dropped his dinner guests. Through the short backyard, over a fence, and across four more yards. He made it to the Harbor Avenue and kept on pumping his long legs.

He was a fugitive for three days before his size caught the gaze of a scrapyard attendant. The brown mop and satellite-dish ears poked over the rear end of a buggered Chevy wagon. Ben Ray Collins, the world's most successful copycat serial killer, received a Louisville Slugger to the back of his head.

The McDonald's worker testified.

KC testified.

The McDonald's worker became a librarian after finishing her diploma program.

KC's fame lent her space to become a small screen actor on nine different sparsely watched CBC television shows before landing a regular spot on an American soap where she played a diner waitress for thirteen seasons before the ghost of her mother's twin sister killed her with rat poison.

1

It was beyond the First Nation land, so technically, it was one of the few *off-limits* fishing spots Leroy and Cal visited regularly. Private land pinched between Provincial Park and band forest, the former Camp Still Waters was ripe with fish.

For years, Camp Still Waters was a spot for the wealthy to enjoy an outdoorsy experience, something to make them feel mannish, to escape the rising steel and concrete walls they loved to hate. Stocked ponds, baited game, and all the bug spray money could buy, the camp was a huge success, but in exploiting the local environment, the owners gained no friends.

American entrepreneurs had no qualms about pissing in somebody else's garden, doubly so since they lived on the far side of the Canadian border. They did not care about the wildlife in British Columbia nor did they care about the people living there. Money was money and money made the world go 'round. Unfortunately for them, two regional judges cared much for the woods, the animals, and the future generations who might want to enjoy that space.

The first accident and resulting settlement nearly killed the business. Six months later, a questionable accident went to court: one guest shot another guest in the foot during a card game. Why had those running the camp permitted firearms where there was alcohol? The alcohol and the handgun were items smuggled illegally when the second-generation Texan oilman flew north hoping to shoot a grizzly bear and catch salmon. The judge decided in favor of the injured and against the businessmen—no matter the legality of the weapon used in the incident or who had true responsibility over it. Camp Still Waters was two years empty and never again was the location to hold a business license without first proving its value for the good of *all* dwelling there.

Leroy and Cal didn't give much thought to the fact they broke rules. The fish in the pond were monstrous and plentiful. Stock a pond and never fish it…*sheee-it.* It would be a waste to ignore all that food.

In this perfect setting, Leroy and Cal sat in a canoe. There were two coolers: one had three good-sized trout, and the other had a dwindling collection of Caribou Genuine 5.5% cans.

"Holy, you feel that?" Cal asked.

"Uh, yeah. Geez, boy, look'it there," Leroy said, pointing a finger to the forest where an old growth elder—probably fifty years dead after three centuries of life—cracked and toppled. The world shook around them. The pond water made a nice cushion for the brunt of the earthquake, but not all of it.

Leroy and Cal were in their forties and lived their entire lives not thirty kilometers from where they sat, never having experienced an earthquake that would shake the dishes from the cabinet. This was something rare and bad.

"LNG and RimRoil, sons of bitches," Leroy said.

Cal nodded. Companies did frack in British Columbia. It was an old fact, but it seemed that recently, these companies had greedy streaks which put shuffling the under layers of the earth into overdrive. The land had begun to shimmy and shake in places that ought to sit firm.

Forever, naturally, the coast had quakes. The ocean is a roughhousing bully. Out in the mainland, amid the mountains, this was a world that had a firm grasp of the planet's core. This quake was man's doing. Surely.

Another tree cracked a few feet off shore and landed on one of the gutted cabins. The locals, Leroy and Cal included, had visited the camp after its closure for bits and pieces once the bank took ownership. A cot frame here, a fishing net there; an outdoor deep-fryer didn't use itself, neither did the gardening tools, or the left-behind couches in the main lodge building.

Some stuff remained, but not much worth a lick.

The snapping and crashing had the birds launching from the treetops. The men and the canoe shifted and swayed, the world was busy, as if dancing. Neither spoke, but both said a silent prayer to Jesus H. for the safety of the Cherokee parked on the logging road up the trail.

Thoughts of the Jeep departed when the pond began bubbling. Great gassy balls invaded the fresh outdoor essence with rotten eggy odors.

"Oh my Lord," Leroy said, then coughed on the poisoned atmosphere.

"Maybe we best get on out of here, eh?" Cal said, sleeve tight to his nose and mouth.

The bubbles continued, though getting much smaller as time

passed. The first fish to float with its pink belly to the sky was a young walleye. The next was a two-foot salmon. Within a minute, there were three-dozen floaters. By the time the fishermen paddled to the shore, the dead creatures counted into triple digits.

The rumble in the forest ceased but for the terrified patter of the local Animalia and the occasional late-falling timber. They tied the canoe to a post driven deep into the muck, then trudged through the knee-high shallows to the shore, each carrying a cooler and a pole. They'd come back later for the boat when the ground settled itself.

A brown bear jogged by them as they scurried up the trail. Overhead, eagles squawked, homes fallen to the forest floor. The deeper into the woods the men went, the less the air wore the eggy scent.

At the clearing, the Jeep was fine, but an enormous branch blocked the lane.

The back gate swung open and they tossed the loaded coolers and rods within. A fresh rumble rattled the men. Arms out, they staggered to the Cherokee's doors and hopped inside. Leaving or staying, that did not matter. Safety was chilling in a steel and fiberglass cage with leather seats and a radio to give them the haps on the scene.

Key turned, music boomed. Leroy switched the stereo to FM and located the nearest CBC station. It was Vancouver idiots talking about kale.

"Try The Brook," Cal said.

Leroy hit seek twice until the digital dial landed on 99.9, The Brook.

"...the reports are limited yet, but it appears primarily localized in the Sasquatch Park region. So, yeah, not the apocalypse like that nut Pauly A. suggests," said the host, Hunter Mike.

Pauly A., still on the line, piped up, "The Lord is cometh!"

"Sure thing, fella," Hunter Mike said. "Now, while we wait—"

"This is the end, sayeth the Lord's...!"

"Cut this clown's line already." There was laughter in the host's words.

It acted as a lozenge to the scared men in the Jeep. Out the window, a coyote prattled across the path. The shaking was down to a hum and the world began to seem like a normal, firm place once again.

They got out, gave a nod, and jogged into the bush. It was only a quick jog to the pond. They portaged on the way back, carrying the boat just as their ancestors had. The trip took nine minutes there and returned. Boat tied to the roof, they stepped to the nose of the Jeep to move the felled limb. It was heavy and the sky overhead opened to let a shower loose. Cal didn't want to say it, but it really had all the telltales of a sign, like maybe they ought to leave the pond alone.

"Man, maybe we stick to our lakes, huh?" Leroy asked.

Since Leroy moved in with Cal twenty years earlier, long before their marriage, they'd mastered a pretty good handle on wordless communication.

"Sounds like maybe that's not such a bad idea," Cal said.

Both believed in signs, though rarely did any incident stick as permanent.

The log on the path was too heavy and the men built a quickie bridge out of other fallen limbs. Half an hour after the planet finally stopped shucking and jiving, the men were on the road. The pond was bad and it might sting the guilt spots if someone else went in there and got sick from whatever that eggy scent was. Got sick or worse.

Home. Leroy glanced at Cal and Cal fished into his pants pocket for his phone and opened the Safari app. They couldn't be quiet about this one.

"Hey, yeah, not sure if I should be talking with you guys or the forest ones," Cal said as Leroy sat across the kitchen table. He got the number of the local municipal offices from Google and the switchboard transferred him to the folks in charge of waterways. "But we was at Camp Still Waters." Paused. "No, I know, and I ain't telling you my name, so listen. There was like a big gas rupture under the lake, everything's dead." Pause. "What was I doing out there?" Cal asked and looked up to Leroy.

Leroy shook his head. "Hang up, don't admit to nothing more."

Cal did as told.

—

Beneath the surface, pressure cracked the honeycomb networks. Water and gasses eroded the semi-natural framework that housed the undiscovered creatures and had most of those with half a brain slinking to the shadows, away from the luminescent greenery they'd basked in for their entire lives. Nothing like this had happened before and their sky was falling. Chambers flooded and the biggest beasts suddenly had space to reach the smaller creatures.

Those not smart enough or fast enough to seek new chambers became lunch. Others yet had the wherewithal to conjure meaning from the changes, especially when their holiest shrine remained unmolested.

Nothing beneath the surface of Camp Still Waters considered the destruction the end of something; all understood that it was something new.

2

It was a mess. Nine inmates of fifteen were off the smallest cellblock in the building, meeting visitors through windows, chatting on the monitored short-range telephones. Over the eighteen years he'd been inside, Ben Ray Collins took a slew of visitor requests, fan mail, hate mail, and lewd long distance calls from bored and horny middle-aged women. The visitors, he ignored. The fan mail, he ignored. The hate mail, he read. The lewd long distance phone calls, he took and stored for later use.

The huge man was a model prisoner. He kept quiet, fell in line, and acted respectfully to every corrections officer, even the scab replacements during the current union strike.

When the world shook, the prison remained firm in all areas aside from a mental capacity. Inmates became like primates. The lifers meeting visitors were already the most dangerous of the bunch and the strike had the corrections crew understaffed. The biggest and strongest men and women manned the general population. Turf wars. Gang wars. Snitch wars.

The lifers hooted and hollered in the dim emergency light that the generators offered. It was a short-lived issue and once the lights returned, a headcount ensued. Every cell on the secluded lifer block had a body leaned against the bars, or in the case of Ben Ray Collins, one in the bed.

As the full power returned, the guards did a headcount of their own and found they had a mystery. An annoying thing, but nothing too far gone, they assumed. A screw-up, they were all new and faking it until they figured out the ins and outs of the prison, so one missing scab guard wasn't likely anything serious. It's not as if they'd lost an inmate.

—

The world was alive with rumbles and Ben Ray Collins stood outside his cell, perhaps on his way to the line for the telephones, perhaps only to exercise his knees. He was the last one on the block aside from the posted guard, a man new to the place that morning. This corrections officer had an overblown top-half and short legs, still, he was nearly six feet. Like a giant potato on two skinny roots.

An idea struck as the floor moved and the power doused. Ben snaked a hand around the officer's jaw, squeezing and dragging the hefty frame. The man flailed and kicked as the serial killer took a chance to up his body count.

The corrections officer's head thumped a wet bang against the cement floor nine times in eighteen seconds. Quickly, the clothes of one man went onto the next. Out of the cell, inmates shouted and screeched. The flicker and shake was a little excitement in the lives of men forced into permanent monotony and it turned them into werewolves drunk on moonshine.

The stolen pants were too short, but the guard's black socks gave the illusion of high boots. The shirt fit perfectly as fat men and muscular men can generally pluck from the same shelves. There was a wallet and a set of keys, personal keys.

Out of the cell hall, sticking to the dimness amid shadows, inmates paraded in like a gaggle of rabid geese. Nobody noticed when Ben slipped out past them. Head down, he walked. The power came back and he quickened the pace. He got to another sliding steel door leading out of his cellblock. A corrections officer sat on a stool, wide-eyed.

"Man, you done your shift?" he asked.

Ben croaked, spitting the first thing that came to mind. "My inhaler," pause, wheeze, "in my," pause, wheeze, "car."

"Oh shit, no problem."

The gate opened and Ben charged through, considering whether or not to kill another guard. He never thought he'd make it so far. This was a whim, a joke, a hint of spice in a dull life going nowhere.

Ben reached a lowercase *t* intersection in the hallway and kept forward.

"Hey!"

Ben stopped, did not turn. His heart thrummed.

"Man, I know. It's a maze, huh? I got lost yesterday. Parking lot is to your right."

Ben turned, patted his chest with his large palm, nodding, and took the hall toward the parking lot. There was another door. It had a card lock. Ben withdrew the guard's wallet from his pocket.

In-between the flaps was the prison key. He slid it through and the keypad lit in pale blue. His heart pounded at a hummingbird's tune. So far, so much farther than he ever imagined…and thwarted by a keypad.

The blue light died. Ben tried the card again. The keypad lit. He tugged on the door. Locked.

"Hey, now, let's play, huh?"

He tried again, same steps, nothing.

His eyes lifted to the ceiling. It was fun, but it was over. The adrenaline coursing his personal track began to clump and suck the life from his arms and legs. He leaned against the door, slid the card again for the fuck of it. It did nothing beyond flashing the blue light. Like riding a bicycle, he opened the wallet and popped the card back inside. Popped it right in front of a scrap of paper taped to the leather.

3366

The keypad remained lit blue yet. Ben Ray Collins typed *3366* and heard the glorious bizz and a weighty click.

It was anything but smooth sailing from there. Through the wings outside gen-pop, past the cafeteria, and into the locker room. There were other guards, he nodded, they nodded, mostly, one didn't. Outside, he reached a fence. An oblivious scab guard opened the gate without questioning the flashed identification photo of the chubby-faced man against the tall muscular figure holding it.

Ben looked at the key fob retrieved from his pocket. It was like living in the future. He'd seen fobs at a distance way back in his glory days, but only rich pricks had them. Sometimes there was stuff on movies too. One guy tried to tell him about the internet once and Ben had to just smile and shake his head. Technology was not in his skillset.

He hit the horn button. A giant Ford truck flared to life. It was horrible.

Wah-wah-wah-wah!

Ben hit the button again, feeling a million sets of eyes on him. The horn silenced. The parking lot was vast, enormous, it was forever to a man that hadn't been in the true outdoors in more than a decade.

Ben climbed into the truck. It was an automatic and came to life when the key turned like a hot knife in butter. The radio played a nasally woman, whining over a heavy pop beat. He turned it down, spying the world, disbelieving. The wheel was loose in his grip. Proper power steering was beyond most of everything he'd ever driven. It was as if the truck skated.

The exit came at him and a tap of the brakes jerked the truck. The last gate. Outside was but a series of chain-links away. The union workers on strike stood around with signs, ready to accost the truck. The gate worker frowned at Ben, eyeing him. There was something not quite…

Protesting corrections officers rushed at the truck. So far, the real employees had been nothing short of a huge pain the ass. The gate opened. The truck rolled out. The guards, some of whom Ben Ray Collins recognized, slapped palms against the fenders and bed. They shouted and taunted. They threatened and Ben's heart leapt in euphoria as he carried on, out the lane, and to a gravel road.

He took a right. His foot pinning the accelerator in excitement. He took a left from there, onto a small highway with a high speed limit posted.

"Hey now, brown cow!" he shouted and punched the ceiling of the truck. When his hand touched on the wheel again, it was too firm, too demanding. The tires shrieked. Black strips trailed him as he slammed the breaks. "Nonono!" Into the ditch. The airbag rocked him backward.

Woozily, Ben Ray Collins, only three kilometers from the prison, climbed from the truck and toward the road.

3

Dr. Dee Grier was up to her elbows in sludge when the shimmer rolled through the ground. From where she was, in the overcrowded lab in West Vancouver, it was hardly a rumble. But there was enough glass on the shelves to shake and rattle, if only momentarily and minutely. Dee lifted her gaze. She had squinty blue eyes and blonde hair. She was thin and short. Old money in revolt, she decided to do something with her life rather than live as her parents had.

"Did you feel that?" Dee asked.

Dr. Melina Carrillo nodded while she carried a box of lake specimens—rocks. Melina stuck out somewhat wherever she went. She was tall, had wavy black hair, light brown skin, the curves of an exotic dancer, and thighs that suggested that she ran for fun. But put her in a lab coat, hairnet, and goggles, she was another peg pulling her weight in a world of men.

"Oh good, I thought maybe that was me. Pretty hungry, figured maybe my guts were gonna shake out of me," Dee said and then her stomach grumbled as if part of a practiced act.

Dee was a biologist. Melina was a geologist.

Somewhere in the lab was the student on placement: Barbie Karimi. Named Bahar at birth, Barbie was a first generation Canadian, also revolting, this against her Iranian upbringing. Luckily, if nothing else stuck, the need for an education remained embedded to her core. Short and tight, avoiding lab coats and hairnets often, Barbie liked attention. She was a research gopher and the recently diploma-ed doctors put up with her because what choice did they have?

Dee and Melina spent the rest of the afternoon speculating on the cause of the quake, but never getting involved enough to step from their tasks to do some lightweight research.

4

Ben Ray Collins stumbled as he climbed from the ditch. His head was a mess inside. Outside, he looked like anybody might after a recent and reasonably soft collision.

An aged Mitsubishi Delica pulled to a stop on the quiet stretch of highway. The driver was a young woman. The van had a right-hand-side steering wheel. This oddity did nothing to assist the man's jarred brain.

"Holy...you okay?" the woman asked. She was bony with a bird-beak nose and a cleft chin. Her hair was a mess and the air coming through the window smelled like marijuana and dirt.

"I need a ride," Ben said.

"Oh, sure, sure. Hop in," the woman said. "I'm Starlita."

Ben swung open the side door and flung himself onto the floor. He slid the door closed with the toes of his right foot.

"Hey, all right. You can sit up here... You want me to call an ambulance?"

"No, please, drive. I need away from here."

"Is it panic? Is it the constriction? I used to sell insurance in an office. It was constricting. Being a prison guard must be constricting."

Ben's heart thump-thumped at this, then remembered the uniform. "I'll never go back," he said.

"I know that feeling. I sold that insurance until one day I straight freaked out. I had to get away. I went and got busy for myself, you know? See my daddy was a hockey player and he used to take me with him. He was a goalie. I love goalies. Well, not goalies, I love the masks, you know? Like, not the cage ones as much, but the old stuff, like what my daddy wore. He backed-up Richard Brodeur for three games in the eighties. The other back-up goalie had the flu. So they called my daddy up, but he never played a game. I kept his jersey though, number forty-nine. Weird goalie number, but it was available, you know?"

Ben Ray Collins was coming around. He lifted himself from the floor and planted on a seat. He remembered Richard Brodeur. The King of the pipes, in Vancouver anyway.

"Really?"

"Yeah, sure. Hey, you're looking better already. That was some truck you crashed; bet it cost a bundle."

"I'm done with it."

"Right on!" Starlita slammed a palm on the steering wheel. "That's far out, starting over from scratch, just like me. I tell everybody, get a van, make art, live for today. Get out of the corporate vice, you know? Freedom, that's the ticket."

"Freedom," Ben said, tasting it, rolling it around his lips and gums. He glanced over his shoulder to the carriage area. There were boxes, all open, with cloth wrapping the items. Everything back there wore a layer of clay dust.

"Hey, reach into any one of those boxes and check out my

work. Be gentle. I sell stuff now and then 'cause I gotta eat, but it's all about people seeing it. Some are exact replicas. Perfect things, right down the leather. I used clay and wire. A puck would destroy'm, but they're not for use. They're my art, you know? My heart, my soul."

Beneath the cloth was the image of Ben's destined continuation. It was as if a lightbulb lit over his shoulders. He picked up a mask. It was heavy and familiar. Out the window, he saw a battered sign for place called Camp Still Waters only eighty kilometers away. Eyes back on the mask. Recognition. Understanding.

"Say, you got a pretty smile," he said.

The woman looked in the mirror, grinned at him.

"I see you have some food…" he said.

"Oh, hey, if you're hungry, eat. I insist, Mother Earth's bounty isn't for me to regulate," Starlita said.

"Or we could have a nice picnic."

The smile widened. Starlita knew fate when she saw it. This was fortune dropped into her lap. It was her calling to help this poor soul through the tough transformation of freedom.

"I love picnics," she said.

"I saw a sign for Camp Still Waters. The sign was old. Who knows, maybe it'd be a nice spot."

"I know that place!" If it wasn't fate, the universe was a trickster, because damned if she hadn't been thinking about the old camp since she got back to the area. Not even half an hour earlier, she'd mentally regaled over her part in swaying the judges when the courts finally bankrupted that nasty operation. She'd petitioned, marched, made art about the evils of capitalism and the destruction of nature. And for once, the good guys won! "Mister, I think it's like destiny that we linked up. I'm gonna help you become free."

Ben rubbed a thumb against the mask. This was destiny indeed. The universe loved chaos and the building blocks of his rebirth were all here for him. Art imitates life. Life imitates art.

Welcome to your second act, Ben Ray Collins.

———

He'd held that mask for the fifty-seven minutes it took to get to the entrance of Camp Still Waters. There, he hopped out, thrilled and excited. The anticipation stirred his manhood, not quite filling the front of the pants he'd stolen, but a stiff breeze in the right direction might push him over the edge. There was a gate forty feet up the lane, into the treeline. He used the tire iron out of the van to crank open the rusty padlock. To the right of the gate was a mossy sign. The rainforest atmosphere did the kind of decay that typically took a decade or more in only a year or two. The sign was rustic wood on wood, tones of dark browns paled to greys.

Starlita had been chatty about her role in the end of this particular business. There was immense pride in this.

She pulled the van through and Ben swung the gate closed. There were three unharmed bunk buildings aside from the main lodge, which was an utter wreck. Dusty glass sparkled on the gravel and in the grass. The air stank. It was something like natural gas, but also something more than that.

"Oh gosh," Starlita said, rain pattering on her shoulders as she gawked at the hundreds of dead things floating in the pond. "Look what they've done."

"Indoor picnic?" Ben asked. He held the groceries and a sleeping bag.

"I guess so. That's so sad." Starlita put her head against Ben's chest. She was a full foot shorter than he was. The top of her head revealed the first strands of grey hair.

Ben kissed the part.

"You feel good," Starlita said. "No wonder you didn't fit as a prison overlord."

They ate in the nearest bunkhouse. Ben tossed two of the thin, rubber-sheathed mattress onto a bedframe after they ate crackers, cheese, and apples.

"I'm going to free you, Ben," she said.

He'd offered his real name, thinking if a memory clicked that he'd murder her without qualms, but doubting it would. This meeting ended in her death anyway, most likely. Though, if she didn't catch it and link it, he'd see how the night played out. Rape wasn't nice. He'd done it in the past to get things right, but moving forward, what he had in mind, had nothing to do with getting off.

Not his getting off.

Not in a sexual sense.

Though if the chance arose…

Starlita reached into the waist of his stolen trousers and stroked. Ben sat back and moaned. It had been so long, he was almost ready to burst immediately.

"They couldn't even give you proper-fitting pants. Are you a picket crosser?" she asked and then whispered, "I'm going to free all the come you've got."

Ben didn't answer the question as Starlita opened his pants, withdrew his cock, and slipped inexpert—but who's complaining?—lips over the tip. Up and down. Up and down. Up and squirt.

"Already?" Starlita gargled a mouthful before swallowing it down.

"I can go more... It's...unexpected," Ben moaned, embarrassed.

Starlita stepped back and began undressing. It had been so damned long she looked like a supermodel, despite the numerous flaws that would never fit a fantasy profile.

"Wow, you sure can." Starlita eyed the almost immediate re-invigoration of Ben's penis.

Once stripped aside from her grey, woolly socks, she pushed Ben back and straddled his face. She smelled of sweat, urine, and fishiness. Ben worked, eating as if he wanted to love this woman. Right then, maybe he did.

The second round lasted much longer and Starlita was satisfied—or close enough to it. She slipped off Ben and scurried to the washroom at the far end of the bunkhouse. Rain and gravity worked the plumbing and that was a nice surprise—a clean-ish toilet and disappearing waste.

Starlita returned and joined Ben on the doubled-up mattresses. They napped.

—

The rain came down outside as if it meant to drown the camp. Ben retracted his arm from beneath Starlita and donned his short pants and corrections shirt. He didn't tuck and buttoned to only one eye beneath his ribs. In the tight shoes, Ben crept from the bunkhouse.

The Jacques Plante recreation was the first and only mask he needed to consider. It wasn't exactly Jason Voorhees, but he'd always added a little hint of personality to every kill he'd imitated. It fit over his face like a second skin. He was home. It was fate. This was his rebirth.

From a rundown shed, he located a splitting axe with a four-pound head. He gave it a swing. Oh yes, this was right, this was good.

—

Starlita awoke alone to a pitch-black room.

"Ben?"

Starlita stood. It was cool and she fumbled around the dark in search of her shirt and pants. In the very heap she'd left them, she found them.

"Ben?"

Dressed, she tapped her toe on the floor looking for her boot. Found one. Found the other. Blind motor skills let her tie the laces.

"Ben, where'd you go?"

The light poured around the gaps of the slightly open door. It was brighter outside than in, if only just. Hands snatching at air and feet shuffling, Starlita made it to the door. The rain stalled her beneath an overhang.

"Ben?" she called out, saw his silhouette twenty-feet away by a rundown shed. "Hey!"

Ben turned.

"Those shouldn't get wet!" she cried out, only an inkling of trouble brewing within. Mostly, she worried over her art. "Are you going to chop firewood?"

Ben breathed a deep helping of clay and woods, and tried to imagine the figure from the three or four of the iconic slasher features he'd seen. The dull paint on the clay began running, staining the collar of his stolen shirt. He took three long strides.

"Ben, why…?" Starlita knew destiny then, doubted it no less than she did earlier. Terrified, she stumbled back to the wall of the bunkhouse. Bumping it brought an understanding of setting and she broke forward, to the van.

Ben raced. He didn't recall if Jason ran. This was real life and running was necessary.

Hand on the driver's door, Starlita glanced back over her shoulder. The axe arced, the heavy head swung down over her.

The axe had long dried. The handle shrank and softened over the years. The four-pound head flew off and through both front door windows of the van. Glass sparkled. The handle struck Starlita and dropped her.

Ben swung back again and aimed the wood at her scalp. Before he struck a third time, he shook his head. No, this was a bore. He ran back to the shed and found a rope. There were expectations to live up to.

Starlita was dead weight at the end of his arm. He dragged her to the edge of the lake's dock and tied the rope to her ankle, quadruple knotted, just in case and because he never was a boy scout.

From the partially toppled lodge, he dug out a cinder block. He raced it to the dock and tied it to the rope, quadruple knots once again.

Starlita was still out. Ben slapped her. He shook her. He nudged her with his boot. It didn't work. He punched her chest and she jerked up like a sleep-disrupted vampire.

She screamed at the image before her. The goalie mask. The pale green eyes. The big hands that lifted a cinder block.

Ben smiled to himself, *now this is a kill.* He threw the block into the pond. Starlita flipped and slid backward, unready to fight the immediate yank. The secondary splash was small. Bubbles surfaced on the black water. Ben watched, feeling wonderful, feeling unrestrained. Starlita was true to her word, she would free him.

No more than two minutes after she went down, a big bubble burped through the surface. More of the eggy scent. Ben turned around and headed back to his new home. He'd stick it out for a while, hide until things cooled enough to take his slasher show on the road, maybe do a few campsites and then switch to a new character.

Who knew?

For now, this was where the heart was.

—

A rush of water collapsed a barrier and broke a new wall. An appendage, not so different from a squid's leg, reached through the hole to explore the cool water. It stretched ten, twenty, thirty feet, feeling rocks and lake bottom, but nothing special. The appendage retracted and the creature forgot about the new hole.

5

The basement apartment shared by Dean Hart and Cody McIntyre was smallish with two bedrooms. The kitchen was a counter space, stove, and refrigerator. The living room was where most of the existing occurred. There was a used NordicTrack treadmill. There was a Gold's bench press. There was a set of nameless, black, steel dumbbells that reached up to seventy-five pounds. There were kettle weights to match the dumbbells, and plate weights, Everlast resistance bands, skipping ropes, a medicine ball, and a yoga ball. There was a shelf loaded with protein powder tubs of various concoctions and labels. There was a forty-inch TV and a green love seat pushed out to the wall, pulling double-duty as jacket rack. There was a steel tray table with a bottle of pills on it. The pill bottle label read *DONEPEZIL*. Neither of these young men had Alzheimer's and what was in that bottle was something called Anavar.

Dean's cellphone rang while he was in the shower. Cody heard and ignored it while he added five packs of Mr. Noodles to a boiling pot.

Naked and wet, Dean broke from the shower to answer his

phone. Cody leaned to hear around the half-wall. They'd seen each other naked a million times before, this was nothing new.

"Hello, Dean speaking?" Dean tapped his foot as he listened, a smile spreading on his face. "Yeah, we can do it. Up to three weeks, sure. A month, no problem."

Cody stepped around the corner, wondering what Dean had planned for him, as there was no doubt whom that *we* concerned.

"Yeah. We love labor stuff. Works all kinds of muscles..." Dean listened, his grin widening. "Yeah, those pictures are real and current. Sure. Tomorrow at ten. We'll be there."

Dean hung up and then tossed his cellphone onto the sofa from where he'd retrieved it. He was five-nine and two-twenty, his skin bronze, his muscles rounded and firm. Cody was an inch taller and nine pounds lighter, but looked nearly the same.

"You found us something?" Cody asked.

It had been a real worry since they'd lost their jobs at the gym.

Life was not going how it should've been going. They met while trying out for the wrestling reality show *Tough Enough*. They had the bulk, but not the moves and went home early, nearly broke. They took jobs at a new gym as trainers. Women liked them at first. They were sexy and had pretty faces, but they were stupid and encouraged the middle-aged mamas to turn that fat into muscle. Encouraged some of the men to seek alternatives and supplements, ones beyond those featured on the gym's sales racks.

"Work for up to a month. Easy labor, camping, chick scientists. The one I talked to looked fine in her email avatar, Indian or something."

"Indian?"

"Named Barbie."

"Barbie?"

The water on the stove boiled over and hissed against the element.

—

It was an in-between season and the email Shawn Romano received was a welcome one. It was a surge to the downtime funding and that was all right by him. He was a hunting and fishing guide that took southerners, city folk, and foreigners on Canadian wilderness treks in the north. He followed every rule and made sure those he led did the same.

His parents had left him a bungalow in the boonies two hours east of Vancouver. It was home three months a year, and this year it appeared to be fewer than that. City scientists needed a guide and maintenance man. Shawn's pal at the local chamber of commerce passed his contact onto the young woman sending out feelers. He hoped like hell that these people weren't complete assholes, though that happened often enough in his line of work.

—

Barbie looked to duck out early. It was her last night in the city, apparently, for up to a month. This was an unwelcome thought. If it wasn't for all the money doctors made, and for her father's firm hand guiding her along to a career as a scientist rather than a plastic surgeon, a psychiatrist, or a TV faux-MD, she'd probably be someplace else. As much as she hated all the work, a piece of her recognized the value of her intelligence and ability to soak information.

Still, she didn't have to like it.

It was possible that the trip might be all right. The doctors had a budget to hire three men. One guide—an outdoorsy type—and two for muscle, should the need for muscle arise. If they had to, there was always the eventual possibility of bringing in machinery, but manual labor was cheaper to start.

Budgets were one thing she hadn't learned much about at school. Budgets molded everything she'd done while on work placement, and did so for the negative in most facets. Saving a dime to the taxpayer in the short run usually cost them two dollars in the long, but she did not make the rules.

"Can I go early? I want to get some stuff done before we hit the sticks," Barbie asked, head popped into the lab shared by Dee and Melina, as well as six visiting temps from Japan who were looking into the radioactive residue spread to the Canadian shores from the Fukushima disaster.

Melina lifted her head from around the laptop where she scrolled through her Facebook feed. She and Dee had called the day early, but stuck around because there was nothing much to leave for and sometimes the receptionists or janitorial people brought in cake or donuts after lunch.

"We're awfully busy. You don't much act like a doctor, did you know that?" Melina said.

Barbie pouted. She hated that these two gave her such a hard time about *everything*.

Dee had a copy of short stories by Joyce Carol Oates in her lap, inadvertently hidden by a tabletop. JCO's fiction had very little to do with biology.

"Look at us. We work hard. We never screw around during business hours. All you seem to do is screw around," Dee said.

They'd already packed most of what they'd need. It was an exciting time in their careers. Though it was a smallish oddity, the dead fish, the gassy scents, and changes in color to some of the nearby foliage was enough to draw the attention of the environment minister. The minister called the university. The university tapped the shoulders of its two most-recent newbies— the cheapest doctors on staff.

It was so exciting in fact, that neither Dee nor Melina were apt to get much of consequence done that morning or afternoon anyway, aside from screwing around and sticking it to Barbie.

"This is bull, you know?" Barbie said, suddenly grave. "I know you read your damned hardcovers and I know you're always on Facebook. I'm not stupid or blind."

Dee was the first to crack and began laughing. Barbie stormed away. Melina smiled and turned her eyes back to the screen: politics, baby, crowdfunding plea, baby, dog, baby, politics, book, baby, gamer score, politics, PhD announcement, new finding, baby, baby, cancer. Facebook was something that rarely varied.

6

Ben awoke on the same cot he'd shared with the late Starlita. Outside, an engine purred nearby. He jumped to his feet. Initially, the mask clung from the moisture, but began drying and adhering to the flesh beneath. An appropriate and agreeable reaction between man and art.

The brunt of the eggy scent was gone from the air. The place smelled like wood and a little like the canned food he'd opened. Tuna and cranberries, a surprisingly tasty combination.

Once he'd unloaded the dead woman's Delica, he drove it on a hiking path and then veered into the shade. There, he buried the vehicle in fallen branches and carpets of moss he pulled from the forest floor. That was afternoons earlier and with each day that passed, Ben's sense of safety blossomed.

An engine nearing was bad news.

He glanced out the closed drapes to a pick-up truck creeping in the laneway. The truck parked and Ben looked at a man who wasn't likely to put up much of a fight when the time came.

Brash action often led to a life behind bars, so he waited.

The bed of the truck had a load of supplies. The man twice

stepped from sight and then back to the truck. He scratched his cheek. He looked where Ben hid and then down the line at the next bunkhouse. Gaze returned, those bulbs burned through the hanging linin. The man stepped toward Ben's spot.

Ben wasn't ready, this was all wrong.

He rushed to the door. There was a lock, but no key.

He gripped the handle and leaned against the wood.

Four seconds, stiff and excited, terrified and ready to explode, the handle gave minute jerks. The pressure against his foot increased. Four seconds, that's all it took before the man outside gave up and moved on.

Ben slackened against the door, waiting. The truck's engine started and Ben rushed to the window, peering through the thin piping of the drape's edge. The truck pulled up to the second bunkhouse and the man began unloading.

—

Shawn Romano had the motto, *work smarter, not harder,* ingrained on his grey matter at a young age. When the first choice was no good, the building trashed, the second door seemed almost as good. When that second door, more likely jammed than locked, did not open, he went to a third door and it opened without any extra effort. It was easily big enough for a work and sleep space.

Being as the trip was a rare combination of both sexes, he decided to try the fourth door. It was a smaller building, a former office. At a steady effort, he cleared everything from the bigger room to the smaller and returned to the open bunkhouse to gather three beds.

The men's cabin didn't have a can, but they'd be all right

using the woods for number one and the women's cabin next door for number two. A man's equipment was made for pissing outside. Not that a woman couldn't handle her business well enough when she wanted to, but having a pecker made it easier to avoid dipping parts into poison ivy. In the end, he doubted any of the impending visitors were of the outdoorsy type.

He straightened everything to a suitable visual and then set up a table. The woman named Barbie said they'd need a sturdy and wide space for work. The extra lighting followed. A row of poseable bulbs on steel arms he'd collected at the instruction of the email. He unloaded the empty bins, leaving them stacked in the corner of the bunkhouse. He wasn't certain what they hoped to find, or store, or take away. That wasn't his concern, so long as they didn't intentionally harm the wildlife, what remained of it, he did not see an issue.

Outside, he took a break. Grass sprouted amid the gravel in irregular intervals. It had a purple hue. The lake was greenish and as he'd never been there before, and did not know the depth, couldn't venture a guess as to whether this coloration was right or wrong. The grass and the trees surrounding the lake, however, those he knew were wrong. The purple was deeper, richer. The weeds remained green, clovers littered the purple mass like leprechaun freckles, and knapweed sprung tall in vibrant lime tones. The scene was unnerving. The dead floaters were a sad waste.

Good thing science was coming to town because shit at Camp Still Waters was not right.

Once the generator found a home beneath an overhang behind the first bunkhouse, Shawn ran extension cords. After that, it was only the liveable stuff. He tried a side door of the main lodge. It screeched open into the pillaged kitchen. Someone gutted the place for all but the cupboard doors.

No good. He'd need to set-up a cook site. It was suddenly a real pain that the one cabin door refused to budge. He got thinking, if he broke the door down, it didn't harm a covered kitchen the way it did to a sleeping area. That was if he couldn't pop that door right back into place.

From the truck bed's cargo locker, Shawn took up a two-pound mini-sledge. Methodically, he tapped the edges around the frame and then twice straight on the door handle. He tried the knob. It turned and the door swung inward, effortlessly. There was a stack of beds in the bed frames in one corner and the leftovers of squatters or campers.

Sleeping near a can was nice, but then again, it was best to have running water for kitchen use. The rainwater tanks held a heavy helping and if he had to hook up a pump to the lake that was an option too. The wreckage next door made the first bunkhouse the prime location for the kitchen.

He made a mental note of everything needed above the norm and turned to leave.

—

Ben made himself small, relatively, and fit behind the door as it pushed inward. He'd stowed away his food, but forgot the emptied cans on the floor. There was no time to reconcile this mistake.

The hammer tapped on wood.

The door glided open and the outdoorsy man in his Carhartts—heavy denims done in khaki tones—stepped in and stood to drink in the space. For minutes this man regarded the room and Ben was at a loss. He could act, smother this man, but then what?

The time wasn't there. It just wasn't right.

The man turned and stepped past. Ben imagined his arms reaching out to grab this man's throat and squeeze until he was only meat and bones.

No, not right. He snatched away his hands prior to contact. He remained hidden until the man moved beyond view. The truck's engine rumbled alive and rolled away. Ben broke for his stowed goods and ran from the bunkhouse.

—

Sixty meters into the bush, east of the lake, the soil next to a massive spruce tree began to move. A squirrel, curious and usually nimble enough to get away with it, chanced approaching the motion.

Balls and misshapen clumps of dirt rolled as the soil began to rise. A green and orange claw breached the surface, and continued breaching. The squirrel backed away, but kept eyes on the thing as more dirt moved aside and a second claw and a pair of beady eyes pancaked between shell halves became visible.

It was a crab. A baby crab, one the size of St. Bernard dog.

The honeycomb tunnels near the crab nest broke and gave room for the smallest of the herd to explore. The crab looked at the squirrel and took a step on shaky legs. The atmosphere was startlingly cold and that had all eight legs and both claws shivering.

The squirrel remained where it was until a familiar shriek rained down from above. The squirrel bolted, but the crab did nothing, stood dumb, unaware that it ought to worry over the cry of a bald eagle.

The bird swooped and slammed claws off the crabs shell. The crab spun and tried to make for the hole, but it had caved in and the crab didn't see any sign of the path—it was so bright topside. Another cry rang out and the eagle swooped again, aiming for the spot it hammered on the first pass. The crack was exceptional; so loud the squirrel crept partway down a tree to have a look.

The crab began maybe an infantile keening. The eagle remained silent before the third strike and was too fast for the swinging claws of the young crab. Through the shell, talons grabbed for meat.

Suddenly the bird was away, the huge crab in its clutches, rising about fifteen feet before losing hold and dropping the crab onto a rock. It smashed and the eagle swooped a fourth time, took a goodly chunk and disappeared from sight.

The squirrel went quickly to investigate, watching for the impending arrival of vultures.

7

"It's so clean," Melina said. She'd been around in the province plenty since coming up as a child, but Vancouver was the center of her universe for the last decade. She rarely left and only once in that time had she gone anywhere that the greenery of nature was predominate over the greys of cement. "I always forget."

Melina drove the Toyota Highlander. A few years old and had obviously received the respect of a rental car: high mileage and creaky shocks, white body with numerous scratches and dents in the paint, and a bumper screaming of inept parking.

They'd been on the road for two hours, she and Dee. Barbie had to pick up the laboring help in her personal car. Her suggestion. It was another half-hour to Camp Still Waters. It had been about ten minutes since they'd seen much of anything but trees.

Dee was a little more familiar with the great outdoors, but still, lab life and city life were the flavors of her existence. As a girl, she camped some. Her parents liked tents, but feared bears, so most times they went camping it was at highly trafficked provincial parks. One year, her parents sent her and her siblings to an *away* camp. Archery, crafts, canoeing, swimming, sleeping outside, pooping in the woods, and knowing what to avoid when it came to selecting the right green toilet paper.

"Not much of a wilderness gal, huh?"

Melina huffed at this. "I'm loving it now. In a day or two, I'll miss my TV. Thank God for cellphones."

"Hopefully there's good service," Dee said, knowing it was unlikely. There'd be bars, but nothing like the speeds known in the city. "Or any service."

"I never even thought about that. I haven't been somewhere without service since...well, the Walmart in the mall doesn't get service in the one corner, unless you hook onto their Wi-Fi."

"That doesn't count. Anyway, everywhere has some service...pretty much everywhere. What worries me is if there's an accident, we're more than an hour from a hospital. I don't even know what the closest town is."

"Barbie will be miserable. At least there's that."

—

Barbie honked at the two men waiting outside the crummy apartment building. She knew without a doubt that she was going to have a great time. These two were all kinds of sexy. When the docs told her to score strong help, they didn't say anything about brains or that they had to look like jerks. These two were yummy and the vacancy behind their eyes made them all the more attractive. Boy toys.

The only real question was whether or not this was going to be a month of work or a month of play?

"Better not be a whole month," she mumbled, thinking no

matter how much she enjoyed looking at this pair, perhaps touching them too, that all good things get old.

Dean won the best of seven rock, paper, scissors contest, and the best of three arm-wrestling series, so he sat shotgun.

"Hey, I'm Dean and that's Cody."

"My lady," Cody said and kissed Barbie's hand.

Oh, this was not going to be all work. These two goofs were enough for a few days' entertainment anyway. A few weeks even.

"We need to stop for some party favors, if that's cool," Dean said.

"Give me the directions. Everyone needs to unwind sometimes," Barbie said, halfway smirk conveying mock disinterest.

They made three stops. The first was a liquor store. The musclemen purchased two flats of Kokanee cans, as well as six liters of hard liquor. Barbie remained quiet, thinking them nuts. They then went to Walmart and Cody ran in to grab three cases of soda: two Coke and one Canada Dry. The last stop was McDonalds. Barbie ordered fries. Cody ordered two Quarter Pounder meals with a Coke. Dean ordered two Big Mac meals, two chocolate shakes on the side.

The car reeked of McDonald's the entire trip. Barbie rode with the windows up, in spite of the scent, so all had equal opportunity to enter into conversation. The men wanted to be wrestlers, TV wrestlers as opposed to the competitive kind. To Barbie, this was perfectly absurd. Of course they wanted to be wrestlers.

When asked about their last job, they both went strangely quiet. Barbie repaired things with chatter about herself and more of what studying a lake was apt to look like.

"Sounds boring," Dean said.

"I'm sure we'll all figure out how to entertain ourselves, and one another," Barbie said, eyes on the road, chest pushed forward, Galaxy S7 on random, offering up some Britney, *Do You Wanna Come Over?*

Indeed.

Perfect.

———

"Look at these two," Dee said, silly grin on her face.

Shawn led the doctors around the camp, getting their feedback on set-up and showing them where he'd put what. He then explained that his plan was to make a hands-on map of the waterways and run-off spots attached to the lake. He had a pack, food, and a waterproof sleeping bag that acted like a personal bio-dome once zipped up.

His vast knowledge thrilled and amazed Melina. He hadn't even graduated high school—though was only short a semester. Education was everything to both the doctors. This man's accomplishments and skills were quite impressive without it.

Conversation about him stopped when the VW rolled in and the giant flesh frames climbed from the little car like circus clowns.

"Hopefully those arms aren't just for show," Shawn said, grinning.

"You want to get them set up with an axe. Maybe you'll have to show them how to… Anyway, we'll need wood for nights and whatnot, yeah? Like a campout?" Dee asked Melina.

"Sounds like fun."

"I didn't see a splitting axe in any of the sheds. There's a hatchet. My guess, someone made off with it. Not a surprise, folks gutted the lodge of pretty well everything metal. Someone coined a few felled trees already, so at least we don't have to bring out the chainsaw. I have a felling axe they can use to chop. Not as quick as a splitting axe, but these boys look like they can probably figure it out."

"I'd hope so."

Shawn stepped toward the lugs as they carted an armload each from the VW. He pointed where they could drop things off and then went to grab his axe.

Barbie held a loaded backpack. She headed for the doctors who stood outside the women's bunk.

"These two sure met all the prerequisites," Melina said.

"What? You said find two strong guys who can swim. You didn't say they had to be ugly, or smart, or anything else. Strong and swim," Barbie said.

"Is that all I said?" Melina asked Dee.

Dee smirked. "I don't know. I wasn't listening. Tell me they speak English at least."

"Sure, vocabulary is limited, but they know all the words to *Don't Stop Believing*. That's got to be worth something," Barbie said. She'd had about enough from these two. She'd never be like them. Sure, they had jobs and did well in the man's game, but they did it with the least finesse and flair possible. "Besides, I get sick of looking at you two all the time, might as well look at something nice for a change. Why would I choose falafel when I can all the meat on the menu?"

"She's got us there. Look at them," Melina said as the men

exited the makeshift boy's bunkhouse and stepped over to the waiting guide. "They're like wrestlers."

At this, Barbie sneered. "Not quite, but they'd like to be."

She walked past the doctors and into the bunkhouse. It was warm inside and smelled like the woods and a hint of eggy air mixed with fishiness. She set her stuff down on a vacant cot and then looked out a window.

"Holy shit," she said upon seeing the purple grass and the collection of dead lake dwellers floating atop the surf.

8

The fire took twenty minutes to light thanks to dampness and the persistent lugs wanting to be *the one* who got it going. Eventually, Shawn took over and a smoldering twig teepee burst into flames. The crack of the first two beers cans came two minutes after that and were generally a bit of a surprise.

After the doctors took quick temperature readings and began the string of on-site tests, the group settled on the idea that tomorrow was another day. The drive had them brain-foggy anyway. The discoloration of the flora surrounding the lake almost certainly had to do with the gassy scent lingering above the water, but it was nothing they'd know by sundown. So instead of the doctors forcing the issue, they handed off the leadership role. Shawn gave a crash lesson in building and maintaining the equipment, piling chopped wood to keep it dry, refuelling the generator, working the campfire cookware, and hanging food to keep pesky bears from taking anything too easily.

"Though if they want it, they'll have it. And if you're in a confrontation with a bear, fight back. They're going to maul you if they have a mind to. Might as well get some licks in. Nose and eyes are your best bet, but I don't recommend getting that close."

Cody scoffed at this.

Shawn lifted his hardened gaze above the dancing orange and green flames. "A full-grown grizzly would carve you like a plate of boiled carrots. Now, if you run into a mountain lion, get big and loud. These ones are skittish and can be intimidated. When in doubt, run for cover. You see a baby bear, run for cover."

"Why would—?" Barbie started to ask.

Melina cut her off. "Mother bears are very protective, right, Mr. Romano?"

"That's right. Now, you run into a Sasquatch, try and get a clear photo."

Nobody laughed at first, and then Shawn laughed, followed by the doctors. The three youngest and least interested, focused on cans of beer. Barbie had accepted a can after the boys had been sipping a while already. It took a minute for them to remember to offer.

While Barbie drank, she pondered the options between the hulks and chose to let nature decide. They'd removed their shirts while they chopped wood. Muscles jutted like marine rope from ship hulls. It was like watching softcore porn. God, they made her horny.

"Anything else we need to worry about?" Dee asked.

Shawn smacked his lips gently as he twisted the lid from an aluminum flask he withdrew from his jacket pocket. "I suppose there is. And maybe it ain't no secret. Are any of you familiar with these parts?"

Nobody spoke.

"Guess it is a sort of secret then. Fifteen years ago, an old man named Arnie Braun owned this land. He was a good fella, mostly, but like everyone, he had his dark parts. See, Arnie was a father. He never married and denied to the day he died that the child belonged to him.

"Take that fifteen years and add another seventeen, and you go all the way back to when Arnie's maid, Dana something, I don't recall what, had a baby named Jane. Everybody knew the baby belonged to Arnie. Dana hardly spoke any English and only left Arnie's mansion to do the shopping. Dana wasn't her real name. Jane wasn't Jane's name either, just what people said because the real names nobody could say right because they were from Tibet. Tibet…? Yeah, Tibet, pretty sure."

"Is there a point to this story?" Barbie asked. She cracked her third can.

Shawn ignored her, stood and began a slow pace. "Anyhow, after baby Jane came out, Arnie paid Dana to go away for two reasons: first, it looked bad on him, so he figured…a rich old man to be fathering the help's bastard-child. And second, that the kid came out all wrong. She had a hydrocephalic head, an under bite, a cleft palate, and nubby arms that ended at the elbows.

"Arnie thought his payoff solved the problem permanently. Arnie was wrong. After a while, he'd get these phone calls at the mansion. Wheezy breathes and a jumbled mouth saying, *Daddy, Daddy*. It went on for years. The *hiss-hiss-Daddy-Daddy-hiss*, every day. He tried changing his number. He stopped answering his intercom. He cancelled his mail service. Nothing worked. Jane's voice found him.

"*Hiss-hiss-Daddy-Daddy-hiss*. So he decided to call it quits on the modern world and moved here. Now back then, these buildings were still trees. There was only one small cabin with a stove, a toilet, and not much else. He'd finally found his peace.

"One night it all changed. Black as tar. A quarter moon in the sky. The gentle breeze fluttered in through the open window. *Hiss-hiss-Daddy-Daddy-hiss*, he heard and shook himself fully awoke. He got up and snapped closed the window, angry now."

Shawn stopped then and turned to face the lake before resuming his tale. "Arnie got back into bed. He closed his eyes and *hiss-hiss-Daddy-Daddy-hiss*. This time when he looked up, he saw her. A near adult; deformed, slobbery, a knife in her hand.

"Old but nimble, Arnie rolled out of his bed and broke for the door. He didn't have time for his boots. Didn't have time for anything. *Hiss-hiss-Daddy-Daddy-hiss*, always the same. Jane chased, stuck on the only words that really got into her hapless brain. *Hiss-hiss-Daddy-Daddy-hiss*. Looking over his shoulder the whole time, he ran to his car. The keys dangled from the ignition. He started it up. Through the radio, he heard *hiss-hiss-Daddy-Daddy-hiss*. Foot down, he roared his Beamer through the woods and back to the highway."

Shawn paused, waiting for the cue.

"Then what?" Cody asked, a half note above a whisper. Enraptured.

"Then he saw Jane on the highway, arms wide open, waiting for him. He jerked the wheel and struck a massive birch tree. The tree survived."

Shawn remained facing the lake, quiet. The next cue came right on time, as it always had.

"And how can you know all this?" Dee asked.

Shawn had worked deft fingers, readying for the moment,

completely unnoticed. He spun and faced the fire, pulling a pale yellow toque sideways on his head and dropping his pants in a single breath. "Because I'm Jane all growed up!" The fire reflected the V of his tucked dick and balls between his legs. The toque was a ballooned lump. His lower jaw hanging forward, forcing his pearly whites out like a pug dog.

Melina screeched as if this was the funniest moment in the history of the universe. The studs laughed. Barbie scoffed, smiling. Dee frowned, sensing the humor, but not really finding it funny.

"Sorry," Shawn said, lifting his Carhartts. "That one kills with everyone when it's all rich dudes, probably because every one of them has maids, and enough of them likely have bastards too." He sat back down and took another swig from his flask.

"That was the best camp story I've ever heard!" Melina said.

"You've never gone camping before," Dee said.

"Then there's no argument," Melina said. "Best. Camp story. Ever."

—

Dee was not the only one missing the joke. From twenty feet into the shadows, the serial killer in a replica goalie mask began again to revel in the wonderment of this new life and the opportunities unveiled before him. If there was a god, it loved chaos, and it loved the terror of creating myths of destruction.

Ben Ray Collins *needed* to do this right. He wanted to be the part rather than only mimic it. Freedom was an aphrodisiac. Resumed duty pushed his senses from an already precarious perch. The beauty of it all made him want to sing.

Singing was wrong. Voicing anything beyond heavy breaths

was not part of the scheme.

"The part," he whispered and took a step backward into thickening bush.

Suddenly like an eel, his tongue danced between his teeth, so he bit down. It hurt wonderfully. Blood spurted. He relented for a heartbeat and then bit down again in the same spot. Hard.

It was difficult to withhold the cries typically invoked in such a glorious agony. He chewed. Blood gushed into his mouth and seeped out at the corners. The deep red trail ran through the breather vent at the front of the mask.

The sensations were immense and then he was through the meaty hunk. He swallowed the third of tongue he'd managed to chew off as if it was a savory chunk of liver. The blood continued to run and he drank, biting down again in an attempt to slow the flow.

He was part of it and like the inspirational monster, he wasn't about to converse with this future victims ever again.

—

As if recognizing that the current number made the hopefully possible impossible, Cody and Dean said their goodnights to Barbie. She remained up late, assuming one of the pair had more will than the other. Probably one was going to be there next to her when the other left. Instead, she was alone, sipping on a flat beer, boiling a puddle of marshmallow on a stone next to the flames. There were other nights upcoming, more than needed, but it didn't take any of the sting away that neither made a move.

They weren't gay, she'd asked, and the way their eyes followed her and Melina, told the same truth their mouths had.

"Ugh," she grunted and rose.

She downed what remained of the can of beer. The last bit was nasty. Shawn had filled a bucket with lake water and left it next to the flames for the last member standing. It was wet everywhere, but it was never wise to leave a fire unattended.

The pit hissed and Barbie whispered, "Daddy-Daddy."

From her pocket, she retrieved her cellphone and swiped it to life. The gentle glow gave her little assistance. Without the fire, generator out for the night, Camp Still Waters was eerily quiet. Far away and all too close, a tree branch snapped. There were grassy tinks of movement.

Barbie quickened her pace. The sound of her feet in the hard dirt and patchy grass rubbed and swished. It was only forty yards from the fire to the bunkhouse. In her haste, she didn't see one of the hoses the doctors had coiled and left on the ground. She stumbled and the footfall sound continued, despite her stoppage.

"Hello?" she said.

—

She was alone.

This was right.

Ben stalked through the dark with long, quiet strides. She picked up speed. So did he. She fell and his heart jumped. The hapless glow of her cellphone screen virtually no good and she had hardly a chance to see him before he was on her.

"Hello?"

Stop! This isn't how! It's too early! You're not ready! Ben spun and sprinted in the opposite direction, back toward the broken-down lodge. There were rules he had to follow. Logic needed its ends nipped and closed.

He slowed to a quick walk, scorning himself for nearly

blowing this gift horse to bits. He looked back over his shoulder and stepped into a hole, falling to his knees. For a moment he sat, only popping up when he heard the rustle of something large moving behind him. Under the moon's shine, he studied the vacated ground, seeing what looked like a trail leading into the basketball-sized hole he'd tripped over. He tried to see down, but it was too dark and the eggy stink wafted up something awful.

9

"Okay, come on out of there," Dee said after checking her watch. They had to be safer than normal, though the lake seemed at PH levels within reason and there were no current signs of obvious poisoning, but something had killed the aquatic life. "Come on now, Cody."

Cody swam to the canoe. He won a best of three rock, paper, scissors contest. Dean was on the shore with a large net, scooping out dead things for collection, and then for removal. If they were going to be in the lake for a while, there was no sense in leaving the deceased fauna floating around.

The boys wore only short, red swimming trunks.

Shawn was off on his trek through the woods. He took maps, his camping gear, and enough food for four good meals. He didn't *need* to sleep in the woods. Aside from Dr. Carrillo, these people didn't seem to like him much, and that was fine; the woods liked him and he liked the woods, so off he'd gone.

"You want me to drag you in?" Cody asked, head and trapezius muscles above the surf.

"Sure," Barbie said.

"No, it's fine," Dee said. "We can paddle."

Barbie shot her a look. Dee rolled her eyes and began paddling. Cody swam to the dock and was already standing under the rainwater shower, scrubbing with a harsh bar soap when the canoe made it back to the mucky shore.

White rubber boots revealed lab fashion rather than everyday use. Dean was barefoot and the pile of dead fish behind him was tremendous. Melina saved numerous samples and was busy at a table, wooden clothespin over her nose, cutting into the rotten fish, seeking out any debris that might be the cause of localized, mass demise. This was make-work. It was something to do until they took the souped-up sonar fish finder out to get a lay of the lake bottom.

That was a day two task.

"So what do we have?" Dee asked.

The pinched nose lifted Melina's voice into an Urkel-esque caricature of her norm. "Not a thing. The fish eat what's there—frogs, other fish, bugs—the frogs eat the bugs, and the bugs are beyond my scope."

Barbie didn't care and went off to talk to the boy toys.

"Do we need someone else in on this too, like a fisheries consultant?" Dee was looking at a scooped-out fish eyeball as she spoke.

Melina plucked the clothespin. "The more the merrier, though I doubt we'll get much, not until we gather and obverse. This isn't normal and it is more serious than initially assumed. The first bunch that investigated, they were with the interior, yeah?"

Dee leaned her left butt cheek on the table next to the fish guts. "Think so? Problem is that whoever called this in got the right person. We wouldn't be out here if it was the average head in the fisheries and wildlife bunch. We're here and there's little help because this is likely a fracking mess."

"Right," Melina said, not entirely following. She paid close attention to what was along her line, but the politics of it all often flew over her head, or perhaps under.

Dee knew this. "RimRoil and LNG had Christina Park and her merry band of money grubbers in pocket. It's always tough to bring any real scientific results against the resource industry, no matter what someone finds. The pretend Liberals in charge often turn eyes away if someone pays."

"But they're gone, right? We have a man now."

"Correct, but half the members are still shills for natural resources."

"Those fucks," Melina said. She'd never voted in the provincial or federal elections.

"That means if we can't figure it out, it'll be a slow road getting anywhere."

"How much do we need then?" Melina asked, gesturing to the mound of dead things.

"Fill a couple bins, I guess. They'll rot anyway. Someone can run them back in the next couple days," Dee said, meaning someone else.

"We'll put the bins in Barbie's car," Melina said, snorted once, and then placed the clip back over her nose. "Want to grab me a couple bins then?"

———

"I didn't think it was going to be this," Dean said, making a disgusted face as he tossed fish onto a lively fire.

Cody shrugged. It was okay. The subject he wanted to cover was the girl, Barbie.

"Are you still, you know…?" he whispered.

Dean lifted his chin. "Huh?"

"I mean, with the girls, are you still not…?"

Dean put his face back down. He went through phases of impotence. Drugs had highs and lows. Lately, he'd been getting eye-fucked a hell of a lot more than fucked-fucked. As nice as that was, functional contact was always nicer.

"What about you?" Dean snapped back. It was a reasonably touchy subject.

"What about me? It only happened to me like three times."

"Yeah, whatever."

"Like, it takes longer than it used to, but it's… Look, I wanna take a run at her, tonight."

Barbie popped up as if out of nowhere. "What are you talking about?" She batted her lashes and pushed out her chest, her hands behind her back.

"Nothing," Cody said, too quickly.

"Go for it," Dean said and then resumed tossing fish carcasses into the fire.

"Go for what?" Barbie asked.

Cody flexed his upper-half and said, "For a walk, once the docs call it a day."

—

Shawn Romano came from a long line of outdoorsy men. His great-great grandfather moved north after deciding the Americas weren't all roses. He sought the vast emptiness and found it. He took a spot on a fishing crew and brought home the bacon via blubber and whale meat. The next generation took the clan inward, hunting bear mostly. The one after that did the same, but lived with one foot tied to civilization. The generation following put Shawn on the horizon. The Canadian wilds and isolation ran in Shawn's veins.

As he walked, he looked for signs of rabbits. He also sought signs of deer and elk. Bears were easy to track because huge mounds of shit don't disappear as readily as the animals themselves. He found none of it and long before the others got to investigating the lake, Shawn started down a freshly trampled trail. Curious. It was obviously made by a vehicle, something moderate in weight, but biggish. The course dodged trees and rocks. Ahead, Shawn saw the curve of a makeshift blind, covering the mysterious ride.

He reached the back of Starlita's Delica and began unraveling the concealment. The moss and branches aside, he peered through the window onto an image that made little sense. He opened the back door.

As the wilderness itself did, the hockey masks touched on memories from childhood. These were old things, decorated in unusual tones and others with odd scenery.

His brother was a hockey fan and had books with pictures of masks like these. Sawchuck, Dryden, Esposito, Hall, Favell, dozens of masks budding up to the late seventies, right before the style made famous in those silly slasher films.

See, that's Glenn Hall. He didn't wear a mask for a long time, but then he did. And here, Dryden only wore this one in the playoffs when he first came up with the team. He's a legend, but quit real early compared to some. Sawchuck, him too, he didn't always...

Shawn smiled at the memory of his enthusiastic older brother, the boy he was before he became a welfare drunk complaining about an injured back that probably wasn't injured and a system keeping him down. He swung the door closed and continued to stare at the masks through the dusty window, another mask floated into view over his shoulder, riding a reflection. Arms lifted high.

Shawn dove sideways as those arms came down.

The axe head in Ben's grip smashed through the glass. He grunted and kicked out at the flailing figure as the heavy steel axe head thumped to the van's floor with the boxed masks, cracking three of them.

"No, wait!" Shawn shouted, backing away so as to avoid another kick. He glanced at the too-short pant legs of the huge figure. "No, I—!"

The big man's foot didn't kick; it stomped onto the hunting guide's back, pinning him to the mossy floor. With his left hand, Ben yanked the steel wiper arm from the back door window and then dropped with all his weight behind his upper body. The steel sunk through the lower portion of Shawn's neck.

Shawn squirmed and screeched. Unlike in the flicks, this was not the end of it. Shawn moved, scurrying on hands and knees toward anything, toward *away*. Ben crawled behind him, grabbed his foot, and reeled in. Shawn flipped and kicked out his right leg, connecting with Ben's jaw, breaking a three-inch sliver of the mask off. Stunned and furious, Ben cried out a guttural groan, spitting bloody saliva all over Shawn as he pulled him tight. The killer thrashed and wrenched, pounding his fists, and twisting the wiper arm. Quickly, blood began to pool.

The dying man's throat bubbled and oozed. The blood was almost black on the forest floor.

It did not make him smile.

It did not make him feel good.

It made Ben ravenous and enraged.

He got to his feet and looked around, wondering where he ought to stick the body when the soil and flora suddenly parted and the body sank from view. Ben stumbled in reverse, blinking hard, thinking he must've found a hellhole—a gas crater—when the body burped back out a few feet left of where it disappeared. Ben stomped with a stretched leg, testing where he wanted to walk. When it seemed solid, he lifted the barely alive body and tossed it onto the roof of the minivan. He then covered the vehicle anew. That was two down in his new kill order, the first wonderful checklist of the modern *him*.

This new him would bat a perfect record. There were five more to kill until he moved on for new pastures and better bodies and he'd get them all.

A kids' camp was the kind of place he foresaw, a place where he might free a hundred little souls. A place where his count and his legend might soar.

10

The sonar system waited on the edge of the detachable portion of the dock. They'd screwed around with canoes for an hour, trying to find equilibrium. The sonar was clumsy and needed a clear view of the water. The canoe didn't have a wide enough stance on the surf so they had to make do with the steady platform.

Strangely, this was Dean's idea and it came while the doctors wrestled and argued with gravity. The beautiful idiot solved the issue and things were ready for the following morning. Until dusk, the doctors and Barbie filled notebooks and a laptop spreadsheet with figures and descriptions. All was normal but for a mysterious standing shape rising from the bottom of the lake as if reaching for the surface but unable to climb any higher.

They marked it as a point to investigate the following day. It was a true peculiarity and didn't really seem shaped like anything—a spike on the map.

The hulks chopped more wood and eventually began drinking, and then wrestling in the grass. The purple hues remained mostly at the tops of the flora. Healthier greens budded beneath as if whatever had come that was bad, had also gone. Still, twice during the day, gassy bubbles the size of exercise balls burst near the center of the lake. The natural gas scent hung around for an hour or so after that. Both Dee and Melina wondered about the scent and the bonfire, but didn't bother mentioning it.

Besides, it smelled like natural gas, but different somehow. Whatever would happen would happen, they were out in an open space after all.

Come day three, Dean and Cody would have to don the scuba gear, once the sonar mapped out the floor. Melina assumed a fissure crack over a gas deposit. Dee assumed something less direct, but to much of the same result. Barbie was not interested in the gas, was more interested in figuring out how to do as little as possible and still appease the doctors enough that they gave her a decent review. The end goal was a job for good money—the shit in the middle was all dues paid.

A cooler evening than the one prior, the fire was bigger and whiskey and vodka went around the circle instead of beer. Even the doctors drank, though for the sake of appearing something like pack mothers, they kept it to minimal amounts. Dee hadn't been drunk for almost a year. Melina hadn't drank with anyone aside from her family since her third year of grad school.

The moon was high and the forest seemed lifeless. Dee was the first to retire for the night. Since the guide was no longer there to bring out silly campfire tales, it was too quiet for comfort, plus the service was too spotty for any kind of cellphone use. It took nearly five minutes for Twitter to load, when it did, but mostly it timed out. Staying awake was just wasting sleeping hours.

The generator continued it hum. Blinds drawn, Dee dropped her cargo pants. She wore slightly baggy white underwear. She flipped off her shirt, leaving on a grey bra: plain, no frills, no emphasis added, and plenty of comfort. White tube socks remained on her feet and she slipped into bulky Roots track pants and a UBC sweater. She'd finished the Oates collection under a steel lamp pointed toward her cot and then swapped it for a Donald Westlake paperback that she picked out of the lost and found from the lunchroom at the lab. It first appeared two months earlier and since nobody took it, she figured nobody was apt to miss it.

The long shadows covering most of the room made it difficult to read, but she managed. *Somebody Owes Me Money* was a hard luck tale, absurd, and wildly entertaining. She read sixty-three pages by the time Melina entered. Melina wore a slight vodka shine to her eyes. She stripped down to matching bra and panties, silky, slinky, red.

Under the sheets, she rolled and hummed enjoyment. "Those boys are borderline."

"Borderline what?" Dee asked, dog-earing her spot.

"Retarded. I know, sorry…intellectually disabled." She burped. "I can't drink anymore. I'm too much of a lightweight. Those boys really did try out to be on wrestling. Like the Hulkster."

"I do wonder how one looks at heavy things and thinks, *Hey, I'd sure like to lift that a thousand times.*"

"Weights are a by-product of a dream, I'd bet. Physical betterment can be addictive. Then it goes nuts and you end up looking like Frankenstein's monster," Melina said and then changed the subject without pretext as her boozy brain flip-flopped. "If that Mr. Romano was here, I'd probably have sex with him. Is that bad?"

Dee was no prude, but she certainly wasn't a demon in the sheets. She'd had sex with three men. Two ex-boyfriends and a one-night-stand in her second year of university, on her first and only tequila Tuesday at the school bar.

"No. He's not my type, but he's intriguing, I suppose. In his way."

"My father used to watch movies in Spanish. Western-type movies, but not so much like Eastwood or John Wayne. Plenty of camping and cattle rustling. Maybe it's some kind of sideways Oedipus thing, but with my dad instead of my mother. Is there a word for that?"

"No idea."

Dee lifted her book. The generator powered down, she frowned, and she set the book on the floor.

"Guess the universe says it's bedtime."

"That or the gasoline burned and nothing means anything," Melina said. "Night, Dee."

"Night."

—

Ben moved aside from notice easily because nobody suspected him there. Only a squirrel watched him as he crept into the women's bunkhouse.

No eyes saw him slide into the shadowy space beneath Melina's cot. The lighting was poor with most of the workbench beams doused. Dee entered and readied for bed. He listened to Dee's breathing and page flipping. She farted twice. Burped once.

She moved around, scratching, adjusting, and fidgeting.

There was a short conversation when Melina finally arrived. She lied down when the light went out. The excitement of his location made it impossible for him to act. He wanted to reach up around the frame and choke her from both sides, but didn't dare. It would set too much in motion and plucking them off unseen was too good.

Perhaps it was possible to kill her silently once the other one slept… It was impossible to deny that it didn't seem like the very best of thoughts. He had to try. It was several long minutes before the breathing switched above him and then across the room.

His meaty hands snaked around Melina. Fingertips touched blanket and then skin.

Gentle breathes rose and fell. Ben let the material reach and depart into his raised palms.

Over and over. A shudder ran his spine and he seethed a deep breath. His hands met the tiny pale hairs of her throat like a whisper.

"Holy shit!" Barbie screeched from outside as a light flashed.

Ben retracted his hands.

Melina sat up.

Dee sat up.

—

They'd been around the fire. Dean off to the side, conceding that his erectile difficulties were probably the biggest player in this game. Like sidelining the superstar with an ankle sprain.

Cody worked his best lines, lurid stuff that sounded like drunk Bazooka Joe jokes. Barbie laughed where necessary, but mostly she wanted to know what Dean's problem was. He'd backed off and really, the game was most fun when the Neanderthals duked it out. If not quite literally, but possibly literally too.

The lake offered so little by way of entertainment and everything smelled like eggs and dead fish and smoke. Cody leaned in and she turned her face. He was wily and planted his lips on her neck. It was okay. She stared at Dean as if to ask if he was really letting this go on.

The lake burped then and while Cody sucked and licked like a pleco fish latched to an aquarium wall, the gas wafted to the fire and lit in a brilliant yellow ball that burned for two seconds.

"Holy shit!" Barbie shouted and jumped back.

Dee rushed outside. The scent was heavy. Melina stepped out behind her. It was already over and the stink was almost null.

"Did it burn?" Dee asked.

The trio by the fire turned and simultaneously said, "Yeah!"

—

Ben came back to the planet from the euphoric cloud he almost let overcome him and recognized the universe throwing him an extension. Rampaging with five still kicking was not a wise way to do things. He had to take care of at least one of burly ones first.

He slipped out behind Melina and sprinted into the woods. Twigs snapped, leaves crunched. He was anything but silent.

—

"Don't forget to dump water on that," Barbie said as she rose.

The doctors had gone inside again. The gassy scent was really killing the mood and the booze wasn't hitting her in the right way.

Cody sulked. Dean smirked, his own sulking through for the night since he wasn't the only one not getting laid.

"I tried, man. You think she's a tease?"

"Maybe she don't like you. It's my turn tomorrow, I think this fresh air is good for my circulation," Dean said.

"What if she wants us both at once?"

"I'll go at her first, then we'll decide, okay, Romeo?"

"Huh?"

"You know, like the movie, *Romeo and Juliet.*"

"Oh, right. Say, you wonder what's going on in the lake. Like it seemed fine, but I had to shower after. You think they'll find something bad?"

Dean huffed. "What're a bunch of broads going to find? They're probably the scouting crew for, like, the real scientists."

"Hey, man, that's not cool. They're mega smart."

"How come I had to suggest using the dock? Most people only think they're smart. See, me, I know I'm smart. You know? I was super smart in school, but I got bored and that's how come I didn't get good grades. Plus I never gived a fuck about osomothensesis, or algebra, or like grammar, or nothing. If I didn't screw up on the turnbuckle with that goof Handy, I'd be in the WWE right now. Probably sucking Charlotte's tits in a champagne room someplace…at least Trish Status' tits," Dean said. "One screw-up, that's all it took."

Cody thought it was more than that. Plus, Cody didn't see why either a famous magazine model or TV star was going to be in a stripper bar. Forget that they might know each other from wrestling, why are they running around with a nobody, even a nobody wrestler? Cody didn't see Dean the way Dean saw Dean.

At the tryouts, Dean was the first one cut. Dean convinced Cody to half-ass protest the next day and then got cut himself. Still, that's what friends do. They take a bullet for each other, that's how Dean described it.

"I know," Cody said. Dean went through this line of reasoning often. "Maybe we should figure out how to do some wrestling again. We could work on moves and shit, then do like the lower ones."

Dean snuffed and spat into the grass. "I'm better than all those shitheads. No, I got a plan. We'll get some money then go to like Texas or Los Angeles or wherever Mr. McMahon lives and we'll like give him a show he can't refuse."

Texas and Los Angeles were not the same place and the plan didn't exactly sound great. It sounded like something a drunk guy that only worked kind of half-assed said and never did.

———

At the bottom of the lake, a giant appendage like an anaconda's tail slunk out from the cracked lake floor and grasped the bloated and floating corpse of Starlita. It dragged the body toward the smallish crack and reefed her through, cinderblock and all.

11

They ate breakfast late. Shawn Romano did not give them a time he'd be back, but the doctors assumed that meant morning. He was an early riser and had a truly workmanlike attitude. To what end did he need to stay away longer than that?

The detached dock floated and worked perfectly for their need. Meticulously, they further mapped depths and activity, or rather, mostly, inactivity. The strange obstacle they'd noted the day before had vanished. Nobody mentioned it, assuming it an erroneous blip and nothing more.

Some of the fish had returned from the river, which was a good sign. It took them nearly to lunch before they got to the spot they really wanted to check. Thoroughness demanded by research did not permit them leave to skip straight to the spot deemed a mysterious potential gold mine of information.

And gold mine it wasn't, but it certainly held tight to its mystery—the fissure, possibly a gateway, which might lead to an answer. The sonar dipped into the crack, but not far enough. Not nearly. The floor of the lake was between eighteen and forty-two feet, all mapped. At the center, where the gas bubbled, the sonar plunked into the abyss below.

The machine was waterproof. Melina wore a wetsuit and a tank. Dean and Cody wore their short-shorts and tanks. The trio donned headlamps. Dean and Cody kept the bulky contraption from falling too fast. Melina guided the way. Barbie and Dee were topside with a rope. Dee was never much of a swimmer—at most, a successful doggy-paddler. Barbie wore her one-piece, ready to jump in if the demand arose.

There were only three sets of scuba gear.

It was murky and dark. Melina had snorkeled enough to be a model for the men, but nothing is easy the first time. Luckily, it wasn't too deep and they had the sonar system clamps on for guidance. They'd fall, simple enough. Rising might be a chore for these two; pure muscle didn't exactly bob. Adversely, that muscle was a good set of tools for use.

They had no microphones so Melina waved and used her headlamp as an attention grabber. Down. Down. Down. It took nearly a minute to get the sonar to the floor. It took two more minutes to get in place over the gap.

From the coloration of the stone beneath her light, Melina recognized the fissure as recent. The hole was big enough for a person, even with a tank, but not for the sonar machine. The read-out was light green on the panel, hardly bright enough to see into the muck. The numbers were incredible. There was great mystery hiding in those depths.

Melina took the hands of both men, gripped them firmly on the sonar, and waved for them to stay put while she went back topside. In seconds, she breached and then snatched the breather from her mouth.

"I need a thermometer on a rope. A long one, like as much rope as we've got."

"Go on," Dee said to Barbie.

Barbie rolled her eyes and then dove into the lake.

"It's deep, like we thought, but more. It's not just a fissure. It's a cavern and keeps going so far that the bottom is beyond the sonar. We should get real divers in here. Underwater cameras. A top of the line sonar. Everything."

Dee frowned. "Who's going to agree to that? Think of the costs."

"Get explorers. This is an unseen cavern. They'll do it for the luxury of being first. Trust me. We can get them. Hell, I know who to call. Wayne Spencer is the guy who heads tourist groups, he'll have all kinds of contacts. I bet I can get someone out here in a day or two. They'll share if we share."

Barbie swished back into the lake with a one-hundred-foot twine on a spindle in hand. One end had a waterproof digital thermometer tied to it. It wasn't going to be exact, but it was enough information to form a semi-educated idea.

The doctors watched Barbie go under and then pop back up at the floating dock.

"The water's warmer than the air, by more than a little," Barbie said as she climbed out. "That's weird. Think it's from the crack?"

Melina pouted her lip. It was the first time Barbie showed any sign of caring. Unfortunately, there was no answer. Yet. Melina pulled down her mask, accepted the thermometer, and dove. Dean and Cody remained in place. They looked bored. It wasn't going to get any better for them.

The one-pound thermometer dropped as Melina let loose the string. Once there was no more to drop, she held it there. The weight of it swayed, meaning it hadn't found bottom. A count in her head took her to six hundred and she wound the thermometer as quickly as possible. She wanted a reading to suggest depth.

She'd have to ask someone, but knowing the temperature was an indicator of how far the cavern might go. Up. Up. Up. The thermometer came into view and the bright red number still many feet away was impossible.

The number dropped steadily as she reeled it in. By the time she pulled it to hand, it was fifty degrees Celsius. Something went wrong. She waited until the number returned to twenty and then dropped it back into hole.

This time she counted to one thousand before dragging it. She got halfway through the spool. The string yanked against her, peeling the outer layers from her palms. Instinct opened her hands and the spool disappeared down the crack.

Trying to calm an imagination while underwater wasn't easy, but she managed. She pointed up after touching Dean and Cody on the shoulders. She tugged the rope twice. The men were slow and clunky. Melina looked over her shoulder often as she swam from the bottom. Something was down there, something that potentially withstood incredible heat.

If that was true, how did something like that get into an inland lake?

—

"Almost certainly a huge bass or trout, possibly it was a frog. You'd go fishing a hundred times and never hook a fish with a mouth big enough to snatch the thermometer like that," Melina said. In the open air, her imagination fell to logic. Logic was the key to science.

All showered aside from Dee. She hadn't gone into the pond past her rubber boots. Thusly, she set the lunch picnic table. Dee was already utterly sick of canned foods. Chef Boyardee was no chef, he was a goofball and master of the overcooked and the under flavored. Still, the two jumbo cans of ravioli went into the pot atop the propane grill. From the cooler, she retrieved the Italian dressing bottle. Kale was indestructible, almost, and lasted the longest of the lettuce substitutes. In a large bowl, she mixed kale, croutons, bacon bits, and dressing.

"Mr. Romano should be back by now, right?" Melina said as she lifted the lid from the ravioli pot and used a large wooden spoon to stir. "What if he hurt himself? Maybe he tripped or something."

"I didn't really think of that. I suppose it's possible he's out there hurt. Probably piss him off more than anything, a guy like that," Dee said.

"Should we go look for him?"

"What about getting divers?"

"We'll send Barbie," Melina said.

"Come on. Look what she brought back the first time," Dee said. "If you don't want to, I guess I'll go. Come back first thing in the morning with troops and anything else I think of."

Dee was already building a list of food to gather. She hadn't thought enough about snacks. If she got a couple more coolers, they could have proper meat. The idea of a stopping by a Vera's for a burger had her mouth watering.

"I'll make the call to Wayne. He'll get some free labor

together for me, I'm sure of it."

"What's happening?" Barbie asked, sopping and sexy as a Sports Illustrated model in her white one-piece.

—

They ate. The lugs licked their plates clean. After lunch, the search party packed two bags and started off down the path into the bush. They missed the tread marks that led to the Delica and the man they sought. They were gone an hour, walking in a straight line through the trees, when Dee finished her list, packed up, and took the lane toward the road. Halfway to the highway, she reached a pile of logs. It made no sense. She got out and looked at the effort. Someone was busy playing a trick. She figured it was Dean and Cody gone stupid on the booze the night prior.

Dee turned back to the vehicle and heard a thump followed by a hiss. The truck quickly leaned toward the passenger's side. A man popped up. He held a machete. Wore a hockey mask. Blood seeped and soaked into the front of the mask and down into the wiry hair of his pale chest beneath a blue button-up.

This was something every girl and woman knew to take seriously thanks to the movies.

Dee broke back in the direction she'd come.

"Help! Dammit, help!" she shouted.

The man jogged behind her, keeping a twenty-foot distance, seemingly in no rush to catch her. Not yet.

She broke past the buildings and stopped at the picnic table, trying to gather a semblance of understanding. She was in the woods, at a lake, and there was a man in an old hockey mask chasing her.

It couldn't be what it appeared. That was insane.

It hit her then. She stumbled onto the second half of a joke. She folded her arms over her chest as the large figure jogged her way. As he drew closer, the joke seemed less obvious. When the machete swung back and nicked her dodging shoulder, the notion of a joke evaporated. This was real and really happening like some wild slasher flick.

Crab walking, she stumbled away from the man, eyes partially blinded by the sun directly overhead. He stomped toward her and she flopped onto her stomach. She tried to get to her feet and the man swung again. Sideways, she tumbled into the shallows of the lake. The wetness was a shock and she rolled in the mud, sliding further into the water.

The man stepped in behind her, his pant cuffs comically dry still a half-inch above the shallow surf. He stopped and she waded out past where her feet touched.

For her, this was slow and difficult. Dee slapped and flopped, paddling to make for the far side of the lake. Every few minutes she glanced back to see the man standing where she'd left him. His steadiness was a wonderful encouragement. Freedom lay only another forty meters to the far shore. Her body fell into an ugly rhythm. She got to a mucky lip and stood, only her head and shoulders above. One last time she looked back.

The man in the mask was gone.

She spun and saw the man running along the shore, racing to the spot where she hoped to exit. Dee made three great lunges, getting within a few feet of land, and then stopped. She turned, already tired, and paddled back out.

The man followed her to his hips, but went no further.

Dee swam. The floating dock was the answer, she'd get there, float a while until the men came back. Dean and Cody had the muscle to take care of this one creep. It didn't matter that he was big and strong himself, or that he loomed like a god.

Charging as fast as her stubby arms and legs dared, she neared the dock. A rope was tied it to its brethren, anchoring them to shore. There was no need to look back, no way he'd waited. The only chance was to beat him there.

She put her hands on the edge of the dock and heavy footfalls thumped an ominous approach.

"No! Please," she moaned, swimming back from the dock.

She waded to near the middle where the gentle bubbling of gas tickled up her pant legs. She'd never been so physically exhausted. It struck her then: to stay in the lake was to die. She had to get to a shore and…try. Try anything.

"Damn you," she said, and spat water as her legs kinked. Her head dipped. A spasm ran through her muscles. Feet moving again, she breached surface and swam for the shore opposite of the buildings, not far from the route the locals used to gain access from the old logging road. "Damn you."

Tears rolled her cheeks, mixing with the lake water. She stood on a mucky ledge and looked up to the shore she'd so ardently driven toward only to find defeat. He was there waiting.

"Why are you doing this?"

The man stepped closer, splashing into the lake.

Dee kicked back and started off for the far shore. At the sixty-two minute mark, she began to bob below with regularity. It was close to three hours in the lake the first time she inhaled a terrible helping of water. Still, she paddled.

Twenty minutes to dusk, Dee picked the shore at the dock and put every drip of energy remaining in her muscles into reaching it. She was stuck in the water, but if she stood, she knew there was hope, and hope was survival.

The dock was before her and her head went down. She bobbed up, tossing handfuls of water behind her. She dipped and swallowed. Bounced up. Only feet from the dock. So close. Down again, this time it was a twenty-second struggle to rise. She reached for the wood and made eye contact with man behind the horrid mask.

A hand like a rain cloud shoved her away.

Dee shook her head. Her body wailed inwardly to let this be over, let her get out, to let her rest. The man behind the mask grunted as she swatted at his hand. He shoved her down and let her bounce back topside.

"Fuck you," she whispered, spitting lake water at him before turning away.

Arms flailing, her mouth fell below. She inhaled. Water invaded and corrupted her lungs.

It was then that Ben Ray Collins decided fun time was over and dropped to his knees, reaching out, ready if this was some haphazard trick. He held her face below the surf, but there was no fight left. The body floated, only the middle of Dee's spine surfaced, like a stubby shark fin pushing through a sopping cotton T-shirt. He grabbed her by the pant waist and pulled her out.

12

Leroy and Cal had begun tracking the seismic activity online. There were websites dedicated to the stuff and related the information in a manner easy to understand. How often their neck of neighborhood really did shake was a real surprise, even if the typical motion came only minutely. People hardly talked about it, but where there was fracking, there were quakes.

It was an intriguing enough fact that the men set off once again for Camp Still Waters. They'd decided to check things over, see if anything had changed, and sniff around for the gassy scents. It was late into the afternoon when they walked the path from the Jeep.

"Whoa, something happening here, huh?" Cal asked from the lip of the lake.

The purpled grass and fallen leaves and needles were off-putting, as if nature finally met a match of some fashion. If only momentarily.

The equipment suggested more than they assumed. Someone official was there checking things out and it didn't look like a resource sapping procedure. This was governmental. Their call had worked.

"Look'it that fella," Leroy said, pointing across the lake to the man stomping away from the rundown lodge.

"Big one. Think this is a government deal, eh?" Cal said, knowing the obvious answer.

They began walking the edge of the lake. It wasn't likely to kill them to go in and check out the scene. Perhaps that big guy was a chatty fellow.

"I reckon it's government, yeah."

It took twelve minutes to reach the dock. They looked into the water, scoping the tools left in piles around the shore. Most was general diving and marine gear, but some of it looked technical and wicked expensive.

———

Melina followed Cody who walked like a man in a bad mood. He had a machete, retrieved from the tool shed. Melina thought there had been two when she popped her head in at their initial arrival, but appeared that her memory was incorrect.

Cody slashed unnecessarily. Branches beyond need met ends. In the rear, Dean and Barbie smacked at bugs and chatted. Barbie *fell* once, right into the big arms of Dean. Melina rolled her eyes. It was a move obvious to all but the thickest-headed men on the planet. Pliable goofs like Cody and Dean were perfect dopes for a woman like Barbie.

Melina was once young, and in her youth, she used her sexiness as a magic wand. The mistreatment eventually came back and the trouble of it was more than her sixteen-year-old self cared to handle. The road ahead narrowed from there. She introverted and discovered her brain was more than an add-on for socially agreeable curves.

Barbie was in for a lesson someday, unhappy marriage maybe, and whether or not it was the kind of lesson worth heeding, only time knew that. Some women get away with everything they want, always, and never meet that one nasty asshole who put his permanent mark on a woman.

At least Barbie had her head about getting an education. The more Melina thought about Barbie, the more she was a mystery. Barbie was only a recurring radar blip however. The hole in the lake had become the main subject of thought, in spite of the girlish laughter and the slashing fury. What was down there was huge and potentially incredible. It was a topic worth her attention and still, Barbie kept forcing her way into Melina's head.

Eventually Melina called out to halt Cody. He dripped sweat and his chest heaved beneath a thin T-shirt featuring a flashy skull and crossbones done in gold latex paint.

"There's no way he's come this way. There's no signs," Melina said.

"Huh?" Cody asked.

"Mr. Romano, remember?" Melina said.

"Oh, right."

Barbie sniggered. Dean wore a wide grin.

"Let's loop back, maybe turn now and then," Melina said.

"Yeah, but how do we find our way out?" Barbie asked, the fun gone from her voice.

"We walked almost straight east. If we walk north and south for a while, we'll either find Mr. Romano or not, but we can follow the sun. Plus, Cody carved a fairly easy-to-follow route. We just have to make sure we don't walk too far in either direction."

"So, what way then?" Cody asked, machete cocked.

"North," Melina said and pointed to be sure her message made it at least partway through his thick skull.

Cody slashed into the long stretches of thin trees. Melina checked her watch often. All four called out *Shawn* or *Mr. Romano* often as they walked. No voices returned. After forty minutes of northbound movement, Melina shifted Cody back west. A half-hour west, then the route shifted south. Cody walked right past his original slashed trail. Melina stopped him and they walked on a northwest angle. It was a bit of a game for Melina. Never did she worry much. The river always ran to the far north and to the south was the cut path. She made mental notes over spillage and pooled waters, wondering if Mr. Romano had done the same and they were out essentially spitting against the wind.

"Okay already, he's not out here," Barbie said.

Cody stopped and looked at Melina. Much of his fire had burned away. It really didn't seem as if the man had been out there at all. No camp, no cut branches, and no bootprints where the river found creeks and mucky swamp patches. It almost seemed as if he'd jetted on them.

"Seems so. Okay, follow the sun," Melina said.

It was another hour before the lake came into view. The entire afternoon was gone, so was much of the evening. They returned at the furthest point from the lodge across the water. The sun was on its way down, reflecting a wonderful pink shine on the lake. It was lucky Barbie called it when she had. Melina hadn't considered the loss of the western marker in the sky, and like many of exceptional intelligence, she assumed some things easier than they were.

"Hey, who are those guys?" Cody asked.

The two men standing on the dock turned around and waved.

—

"Looks like they skipped off the reservation," Dean whispered.

"Chief Flannel Shirt and Chief Getting Drunk Later," Cody said back, despite the fact that he'd likely get drunk later. "Must've lost their casino."

Neither Barbie nor Melina heard this as they walked toward the men. The lake burped another fantastic belch of gas. The air instantly putrefied.

"You guys with an oil company or the government?" Leroy asked.

"Or both?" Cal added.

"I'm Dr. Carrillo, this is Barbie Karimi, and those are service monkeys," Melina said. "Can we help you with something?"

"Uh, no. Just checking in. Been watching the earthquake stats on the internet," Cal said. "Thought we'd take a peek around the neighborhood."

"Okay," Barbie said, tone snide.

"You trying to find what happened to the grass, where that gas comes from and all that?" Leroy asked.

Melina nodded. They weren't on a secret mission, but it was better to share findings once they'd mapped every corner.

"So, what's going on?" Cal asked.

"Can't say for sure. There was some movement in the lakebed, beyond that we have nothing," Melina said, almost apologetic in tone. "In a few weeks we'll know more."

"Staying for a while then?" Leroy said. Not that he was ready to start fishing at Still Waters again, not any time soon.

Melina nodded and then a thought struck. "Hey, we're looking for a member of our crew. Have you seen anyone else out here?"

"Sure, a fella, big guy, well, not big like these two, but bigger than us," Leroy said.

"He was farting around across the lake. Then he didn't come back around. We were about to call for him when you came up," Cal said.

"What a relief, huh?" Melina turned to Barbie and then to the dynamically dull duo. None seemed to care one way or the other. "I guess I better go check in. Hopefully he didn't run off again. You fellas come in by the road?"

"No. Trail over yonder," Cal said.

"Good, if you're still worried about the lake, stop in sometime later in the month," Melina said. It was a move she observed once at a dinner party. Nosy neighbor and unwelcome guest turned around at the door before they really understood the host turned them around at the door. "Have a nice evening."

Barbie grinned and then followed Melina around the edge of the lake. Dean and Cody put their arms over their chests and flexed as if these two soft middle-aged men were in the mood to rumble or overstay their welcome.

Leroy gave a salute to the big men and took Cal's hand. They headed along to the trail they took in.

—

Cal's tummy rumbled as they walked. It was suppertime according to the internal clock. Once into the clearing, the

Cherokee came into view. Soon after, the scent of gasoline joined the vision.

"What the fuck?" Leroy asked, charging to the rear end of the vehicle.

Glass littered the ground like fallen stars. The chemical stink was heavier up close. Cal looked in the bush around him for the culprit.

"Who would do this?" he asked. Every panel had dents. The fenders had axe holes. "This is—" he started to add that the situation was nuts, but a flame burst alight inside the vehicle.

Leroy skidded back at the bright flare. His hands rose to cover his face. A familiar *buzz* filled the air.

His jacket tugged forward.

The fishing reel buzzing slowed. He stumbled, chasing it toward the pyre.

Dug into his jacket's chest and the suspenders beneath was a familiar fishing gimmick. The Monarch Hook was a cheater's lure. At the base were duel regular hooks. At the top was a four-point, spring-loaded system that drove jagged barbs home on contact with a fish. Leroy hadn't used this hook in years, and still, he left it in his tackle box because, although he it bought as a gag to show off, it did cost money. The tackle box stayed in the back of the Cherokee all year 'round.

Leroy tugged at the hook that grabbed his flannel coat like a pitbull on a steak.

"No, wait," he said, stupidly. He stumbled and tripped, his upper-half pitched into the tailgate. Another yank, the flailing man's head cleared the broken rear window. The flames licked up his chest from the destroyed floor over the hacked-open gas tank below. "Cal!"

Movement was beyond Cal. What was before him was impossible. It was the kind of absurd terror from campfire tales. If someone wanted to hurt someone, they hurt them, creativity in the act hardly mattered.

The buzzing continued, slow and steady, as if the figure on the far end of the line fought a man as if he was a marlin. Leroy screamed as his frame wrenched up and into the back of the Jeep. He bounced and writhed in the flames. The reeling sound was no more and he climbed backward the way he'd entered. Flaming gasoline dripped in his wake. He was a crawling fireball.

"Cal!" Fire shot up his throat as if he'd swallowed fuel, burning away the fumes within his chest. His right hand reached. "Cal!"

Cal, heartbroken, fell to his knees. Fire be damned, he wrapped his arms around Leroy in a pitiful attempt to quell the screams, suffocate the flames.

"Roll. Roll," Cal said, tears spilling. The flames burned his neck and his hair lit beneath his Blazers ball cap. "Roll."

They rolled.

Ben Ray Collins stood atop the Jeep watching this hapless display, waiting. Cal's gaze finally turned, catching full sight of the man who they'd seen across the lake. The mask drove a new spike of terror through him as he finally let go of Leroy.

Singed and blackened, his denim jacket and pants kept most of the burns superficial—neck and scalp excluded; they were a touch crispier.

Cal kicked backward as Ben jumped down, his bootlaces flaring with little bursts of light before melting into a mush. He stepped slowly, moving only twice as quickly as the figure on the ground. It was all for the delightful ambience of destruction. In his right hand was the machete from the Camp Still Waters tool shed. In his left was the club Cal and Leroy took on fishing trips. The club had old fish guts clung to it. Blood speckled it front tip to base.

"No, wait," Cal said, lifting his arm.

The first blow came down and snapped Cal's forearm, giving him an extra elbow. He howled and rolled to his side. Ben swung back and aimed for the bean on the top of the man's ball cap. Within three fluid swipes, blood spraying as if splashed from a puddle, Cal was a soulless meat lump. Ben dropped the club and dragged Cal by the foot to the Jeep.

He tossed him through the back window. Ben repeated this with Leroy, who was alive yet. Temporarily.

There were four more lives beyond these two—he considered them a bonus pairing—to end before he moved on. In prison, he'd forgotten the thrill of the kill, but he had it in his grasp and never again would he let it loose from his grip.

13

Cody started the fire and helped Melina ready a meal. It was obvious that he'd turned his sights onto a new target. Melina was neither flattered nor surprised. The man was young and his headspace was that of a hound dog trailing a bitch in heat. Too bad for him, he was all the wrong flavors of brawniness.

Next to the fire, Dean made his move. He put a hand on Barbie's leg and she let it sit there. Emboldened by this, he leaned in and stuck his tongue in her mouth.

She backed away and said, "Get us some drinks, huh?"

They ate camp dogs with kale salads. For desert, they shared a bag of Oreos. Despite zero signs of reciprocation, or interest, Cody kept at Melina until after agreeing to top up her sparkling water with vodka when she suggested that he stop if he wanted to keep his job. Cody needed his rent money and what little brain he had, came back to him.

"Oh, shit, right," he said.

Dean continued pawing. Barbie permitted it, but only in bits. She often glanced back at Cody, wanton eyes.

"You're a cold woman," Melina whispered, drinking the

scene.

"What's that?" Barbie asked from across the fire.

"I wish we had a stereo," Melina said.

"We could use a phone. Or there's a wind-up radio in our bunk. It's in the little part where all the old stuff's sitting," Cody said.

"Oh," Melina said.

Cody shot to his feet as if ordered to do so. He couldn't lose another job and once this posting didn't need him, he thought he might reconsider his role as Dean's sidekick. Might. That meant covering the whole sum of a due rent.

In the bunkhouse, he flicked the light switch. Nothing happened. He flicked it again. Nothing. In the dim shadows, he stepped across the mostly bare floor and to the back room. It was darker. He pushed open the drapes on the small window and looked around for the radio. He was certain it was there. Each shape stretched inches above itself with the low-level flicker of firelight coming through the glass. The objects became like a miniature cityscape, rectangles and triangles rising into the dark sky.

Orange danced against grey on the desk, behind a dead lamp, and against the panel wall. Cody took the radio and turned on a pivot. Bounding, he rushed out of the bunkhouse.

It felt for a heartbeat or two as if someone was there with him. The sensation was eerie. Though not normally paranoid, his size was usually enough of a warning to those apt to fuck around, something about the lake and the rundown cabins gave him the heebie jeebies. At the door, he turned left, never seeing the figure trailing him to the right. Cody peeked over a shoulder to the corner where the warm light of the fire reached. Nothing.

He cranked the arm on the rear casing of the radio while he walked the remainder of the trip. The box hissed and he fingered the wheel on the top until landing on a rock station. Nickelback, his favorite. Their shit always pumped him up.

Melina didn't look at him when he returned. He set the radio next to the fire and then grabbed another beer. If nobody cared what he did, he might as well get stinking drunk.

Barbie pushed Dean, playfully, and then hopped to her feet. "Swimming, anyone?"

There was no time to answer before she began stripping down. Melina considered reminding her of the potential for contaminants, new fish dwelling therein or not. Barbie was drunk and *heard* nobody anyway, so to hell with it. Down to a bra and thong. The bra fell away, the thong rolled to her ankles.

"Coming?" She glanced back to Dean.

Any reason to strip and Dean was ready. Anything more might prove troublesome, but looking ready demanded nothing more than what he'd prepared for. His life was a series of steps on the way to baring skin.

Melina watched his shadowy balls from behind, the tip of his penis bouncing as he ran. It was idiotic and juvenile, and still she buried laughter in her shoulder. Human penises and testicles were a joke of nature. Cody stood with a beer can in hand and Melina assumed he'd chug the beer and then strip. Instead, he went to the cooler, withdrew a bottle of rye and twisted the cap. The cap when into the fire for emphasis.

Cody lifted the glass bottle to his lips and took a long slug. It was going to be an ugly night, probably. Melina suddenly wished for Dee's return. Despite knowing she wouldn't be back until the following morning…morning at the latest, she hoped.

Melina rarely grew lonely at home. She lived alone, but she had her computer, had the television, and had the bright lights out the window. The bush was a lonely place. For a tick, she entertained the idea of using Cody to fill some time and then scoffed. She poured out the remainder of her drink and leaned back to listen to the band on the radio, a song she'd never heard by some dudes that sounded like most other mediocre rockers.

—

"So, how'd you win out on the lottery?"

Dean smiled. Dumb, sure, but what she said meant he was going to get laid, should the trains all run on time.

"I'm the real alpha, obviously," he said. "Cody's cool and everything, but he ain't me."

Dean swam until Barbie was within reach. He latched on. Her legs went around his hips and the warmth on his thigh sent shivers everywhere but to his cock. The game was in the early stages yet and chicks liked foreplay anyhow. So, no issue, only primary warning signals. There was time yet to stand for attendance.

Barbie traced a finger down his chest. Dean leaned in and kissed her willing mouth. His lips roved her neck, to her chest. The moonlight overhead silhouetted them on the lake like featherless midnight ducks.

—

"Well, that's enough porn for me," Melina said. She stood, brushed off the seat of her pants, and stepped to the bunkhouse.

Cody sipped the rye like it was beer. Big as he was, it took a goodly sum of liquor to put him down and he planned to take every ounce it demanded. This shit was fucked. He was supposed to get Barbie. Dean always did this and then blew it anyway with his limp dick. He did too much with the supplements and additives—'roids.

"Enjoy his wet noodle, you fucking slut," Cody slurred and tipped back.

—

The lake burped three times causing three delayed flame flashes above the fire pit.

"Ugh, holy that stinks," Barbie said and then swam for shore, leaving Dean behind.

For much of the time swimming, he grabbed himself, tugged, squeezed, and rubbed, trying to bring his equipment to life. So far, he thought maybe something was starting, a hint of more to come.

Cody watched Barbie climb out naked. She was trim and her brown skin glowed as the dripping lake water banked the fire light. Her nipples were like pebbles and her pussy was shaved smooth. Cody was immediately hard. She walked to the shower stall, flashing a grin on her way by.

Dean climbed out and followed her.

The lake farted a double blast and the eggy scent was horrid. It mixed poorly with Cody's erection and he decided, drunkenly, that perhaps the doctor wanted him to come to her bed. Some women wanted to look like prudes but deep down were straight demons.

The generator was off for the night and Cody stumbled along in the dark. As his best chance with any woman was thanks to his figure, he stripped naked. His hard banana-shaped penis bounced like a dancing marionette as he walked. In through the door, he crept to Melina's bedside. Looming, he wasn't sure how to approach the attempt, so he stood there, waiting.

More than a minute passed and his cock began softening. He started rubbing it gently. Firming, he forgot himself and stroked faster.

Melina awoke. "What in the hell are you doing?" she shouted.

Cody shook back to the moment, recognizing what it looked like. "No, I was… It was going soft and I wanted you to… It's good. You wanted me to come in here, right?"

"What in the fuck are you talking about?"

"I…I love you," he said.

"You stupid ass. Get out!" Melina fought a smile.

"No, okay, I don't…but, like, we can have sex or I can finger you or something," Cody rambled, his words stumbled together like the bodies of a zombie mob on Black Friday.

"I don't want to have sex with you," Melina said, her smile fading. He was a big man and she was already on her back. And he was drunk. "Please, leave. It's okay that you find me attractive, but you've got to…I'm…umm…I'm on my rag."

"Your rag?"

"Yeah, I'm bleeding like crazy. There's bits of dead uterus lining coming out too. It's a bad one."

"Oh, gross," Cody said and then turned around, ambling to the door and through.

He left it open. The eggy scent wafted into the bunkhouse and Melina sat up. The lake rumbled four times in quick succession. Flame touched gas cloud and burst in spectacular shows of nature.

Melina heard no more of her late-night visitor.

—

Cody didn't make it far and faced the woods. He spat on his hand and started jerking with emphasis. He closed his eyes and thought of Barbie's body and, strangely, of Melina's talk of period contents.

—

Ben Ray Collins watched from the tool shed. It would be an opportune time to take this man out, but it wasn't right. Spending so many years in prison, Ben appreciated the act of self-love, or, at very least, self-expulsion.

—

Barbie and Dean stepped around the women's bunkhouse as Cody pulled his discarded shirt back over his head. Barbie said something about the fire that he didn't quite catch. Dean wore a wide, yet worried grin that flashed in the moonlight. They stepped into the men's bunkhouse and out of Cody's view.

Rather than dwell on his failures in the dark, Cody returned to the fire. The half-finished bottle of rye sat next to a bench log. He settled on the ground and picked up the bottle. He sucked back, letting the liquor wash away the pain of singularity and inadequacy. He drank until he vomited. The bottle had only a dribble remaining. To cleanse the nasty flavor in his mouth, he lifted and tilted. The burn was good.

Lying on his back, Cody held the bottle, eyes closed, sucking the last drops into his puke-rotten mouth. The bottle slipped and the neck slammed his uvula. He tried to push it away, but there was force, immediate and powerful. The long neck of the bottle drove deeper and Cody choked and squirmed.

A foot pressed down on his chest. He fought the bottle and the hands pressing it home. He swung a fist and the glass shattered. The warmth of blood coated his arms and chest. The pressure continued, though different. The broken body of the bottle carved into the meat of his face. Blood gushed then. His lips disconnected and he screamed shards of terror into a bevelled recyclable symbol at the base of the bottle, like the war cry of a firefly in a jar.

Deeper, the bottle ground until bone met thick, sturdy glass. Still, Cody tried to fight, but was too frantic to do much more than swat and shake. Blood choked and pink snot bubbled from his nostrils. Through the blood running up into his stinging eyes, Cody stared into the gaze of a man in a hockey mask. It was the single worst image one could see while camping at a lake. He screamed again, gargling on the slicing flow and crystalline slivers.

The man above then leaned harder and Cody understood what had happened so far was mere foreplay. The pressure increased as the figure leapt down, elbows locked straight. The bottle base cut while the pressure broke bones, muscles, tendons, flesh, and into the grass behind his head.

Cody stopped moving.

Cody's leg began a steady twitch that lasted for nineteen seconds.

The lake rumbled an enormous burst and the ball that hit flame was immense.

Ben fell sideways, not expecting this. Great splashes followed. The flame hit the gas and shed light over the lake.

Long, skinny appendages darted above the surface and sank below like wriggling peek-a-boo fingers.

Ben Ray Collins blinked. No time to dwell, the show was live and it must go on.

—

"Aren't you going to fuck me?" Barbie said.

"I'm not done yet. Just let me do this for you," Dean said.

His face buried in shaved pussy, he went to town like a toddler with a bowl ice cream. It took some effort and his mouth was sore already. Dean had his hand on his cock, and finally, finally the blood began to pool. On top of this, Barbie began to buck and squeal. He kept licking, knowing frantic legs were the sign of a happy gal.

—

There were almost limitless options for the kill.

Since seeing the long, coiling fin on a steel shaft of a manual ice auger in the tool shed amid all the fishing junk, Ben had a plan for it. The lapping fuck sounds filled the bunkhouse. Ben entered and strode quietly, though quickly. The auger was three-feet tall and worked like a Mennonite's hand drill.

Ben stood over Barbie's head, waiting for her to open her eyes. They did and she screamed. The auger tip drove into her throat and cut through the meat in three swings of the wrist. Her body convulsed as her spine lost track of messages from the brain. The twenty-nine-inch bit continued to spin, down through the bed. It reached the floor and bit in to steady the dead body and Ben let go, the handle stopping its motion just before reaching the victim's dislocated chin.

—

Finally ready and willing, Dean was rock hard and lifted his head. Here was a man about to use something that had gone unused for too damned long. Not drunk—booze made it more difficult to find firmness—Dean had his feet beneath him when he jumped back.

"What the fuck?" he shouted.

Ben lifted his head, heavy steps and stable in self-assuredness. The blow Dean gave to his forehead was unexpected and incredible. The top of the mask cracked and a V-shape broke free an inch above his eyebrows. The machete was beneath him on the floor and he swung it out before Dean had a chance to land another strike.

"Oh shit," Dean said and broke away, his erection already deflating. "Cody! Cody!" he shouted once outside.

———

Melina was up and watching the lake rumble to life through the bunkhouse window. Just out of view was Cody's corpse. She hadn't heard him over the tinny radio sounds and by the time the crank ran out of juice, he was already a slab of meat.

There were new sounds. She ran to the door and slipped into her sneakers when she heard Dean shout for Cody. The first thought was that he mistakenly hurt Barbie and needed help to clean up a mess. It was unfair, but there was fear and panic in that voice.

"What's happening?" Melina shouted and chased after Dean.

He ran to the last known whereabouts of his good pal. He screamed again, this time in a wordless shriek. Melina closed in behind him.

"Dean? What happen—? Oh dear God!" she said seeing the

destroyed man.

Dean paced, naked. The lake behind him rumbled almost constantly.

"There's a guy in like a Freddy hockey mask," Dean said. "He killed Barbie."

Melina wanted to correct him. Freddy was a nightmare bound pervert and Jason Voorhees wore the mask. She didn't, it was all too impossible.

"Look out!" Dean shouted.

Ben approached, cocking back his machete. The ground quaked beneath them, sending all three tumbling. Melina crawled two feet before scurrying upright and further away from Ben. Dean was behind her and spun her shoulder.

"Come on," he said and began jogging.

To his surprise, the man in the mask ran too.

"Fuck!" Dean picked up pace and Melina trailed behind him. Her frame worked best with distance, but she was in shape and had the muscles to move when necessary.

"We need a phone! We need the police!" Dean said.

"The lab," Melina said and they rounded the bunkhouse-cum-laboratory.

Melina screamed and fell to the ground. Dee's corpse hung from her wrists, head, and feet. Large spikes driven home and holding firm around the frame. Her eyes were half-sleepy slits and her jaw dangled in a dead yawn. Her hair was damp and stringy in the moonlight.

Dean stumbled away, stepping over Melina. He shook his head and rubbed his giant forearms. "No. Nope," he said.

"Why would someone do this?" Melina cried into her palms.

Dean paced back and forth, flexing his hands. He was fury pent and ready to explode.

"Come on, you fuck!" Dean shouted into the darkness around them.

The masked man was nowhere.

Dean continued pacing, spying the treeline while Melina worked through a series of mental snapshots. She'd known Dee for years. Dee was a real friend in a world where Melina didn't have a great number of friends. In fact, since taking her position, she'd really only had Dee, maybe one or two others in the lab, but nothing as close as she was to Dee.

"Why?" she cried out. "You prick, why?"

It was darkness everywhere that the moon did not touch. The light covered most of the general vicinity, but neither Dean nor Melina saw the huge loop of rope on the ground amid the shadowy gravel and dirt driveway.

Dean stopped pacing. "Come out, you pussy!"

The rope reeled into the black woods. The loop bumped into Dean's bare heels. He looked down, startled by the touch. The noose cinched tight in a flash and his feet jerked out from beneath him.

———

Melina cowered in the shadows next to the lab. She watched and waited for something to happen. Dean whined and made demands, screaming for her to help him. She didn't dare try anything.

The lake rumbled louder than before, releasing burps and farts of noxious gas in continual, irregular reports. Twice more the ground shook underneath her feet.

"You've got to do something," she whispered and crawled to a window. She couldn't face maneuvering around Dee. That wasn't within her abilities. "Come on. Come on," she grunted as she shook the window in its wooden frame. It squeaked up and she climbed inside.

Using her hands as eyes, she sought with a vague memory for recollection. It was there. On the table. As it had been, off and on, since they arrived, there were no bars within the buildings. "Shit," she hissed and crouch-walked to the window she'd come through. She didn't want to go back out there, but maybe if she stuck her arm out...

"Get me down!" Dean shouted.

Out of the shadows like a nightmare flash, the man in the mask streaked across the parking lot. He swung the machete in a tomahawk arc and cut into Dean's forearm. The meat of his hand and wrist dangled by tendons and muscles. The broken bones shined like mirrors in the moon glow.

Dean howled.

Melina screamed. She dialed nine-one-one.

It connected and she brought the phone to her face, back inside. The call dropped. Another flash streaked across the lot under Dean. The machete swung in a reverse tomahawk, slicing into Dean's left wrist and hand as he held the destroyed sum of his right. It split like a wishbone. Suddenly, his palm was doubly wide.

Dean's roars rang anew as he thrashed with pain. Melina dropped down to put the man out of view. She waited and cried. It was a battle and she didn't care for that. In life, she prepared and researched, her daily battles met an everyday conqueror. This was too much.

"Please. Doctor, Melina, please. Help me."

Melina covered her ears and shook her head.

"You gotta help me. Oh Christ, this hurts, please. Doctor Carrillo, come on. Get me down."

Minutes mounted and she was unable to deny it any longer. She looked at Dean. There was a trickled puddle beneath him on the driveway. He was pale and his expression revealed a broken man.

Melina reached the phone out the window once again. She connected. There was movement by the door. She started into a haphazard description of Camp Still Waters. The motion shifted to behind her. Machete raised, Melina turned around and shrieked.

The floor shook. The biggest quake yet. Ben fell. The cellphone dropped from Melina's grasp, losing its connection to the nine-one-one operator.

A hand wrapped around her ankle.

"No!"

A second hand grabbed her left arm. Ben lifted Melina and tossed her through the open window. She landed with a thud.

The earth rattled, and crack-cries filled the air, the eggy scent a thick fog. Ben stepped through the dark bunkhouse lab and outside. Dee lay on the ground, cast away, her job done. The last woman wasn't playing her role well enough. A weakling for the spot of final girl was apt to take much of the fun from the scene. Real life wasn't like movies. More often than not, the bad guy won, and easily.

14

Revelling in it all. He'd put women in cages, men down holes, he'd disintegrated flesh in barrels, and he'd flayed and patched together human meat. There were bodies in his yard, or rather, there had been before the cops dug them up. Bodies floated, bodies sunk, he'd tossed bodies away in little chunks around the city. He'd kidnapped, tormented, mind-fucked, and caressed helpless impending corpses, but the woods...this was where he thrived.

Ben Ray Collins had never felt so himself.

Ben Ray Collins was making art come to death.

He lifted Melina by the damp mop of curly hair, stringy with terror sweat. The machete touched her skin. He kneed her shoulder and jerked her head by a handful of threads, her scalp losing grip on dozens of strands. Awake, the best way to die.

The ground shook anew. It was incredible, like a cannon boom. A cracking din echoed over the trees. Ben went still. Dean wailed. Melina opened her tear-smeary eyes.

She screeched music and Ben hummed along. He reeled back

with the machete. Beheadings weren't as simple as TV made them seem—what was?—but he'd give it what he had and if it didn't work with a single, clean stroke, there were always more room for another try.

The ground shook harder and Ben stumbled again. Melina tipped onto her side. Ben would've cursed, had he the equipment to do so. Instead, he groaned.

The parking lot cracked. The eggy scent poured forth like sea fog. Dim green fissures snaked and spread. The glow was faint, but coated Dean like TV backwash. His face went from Ben to Melina to whatever mystery dwelled within that hole. "Help!" Dean shouted, reinvigorated.

A slender, green, tail-like appendage slashed upward, reaching above Dean and grabbing for the steady branch.

"God, no!" Dean wailed, his torture forgotten.

The branch bent and the appendage curled. A second limb slapped against the parking lot. Green algae mucked and sloshed beneath its reach as it slid in search of purchase. It found the bunkhouse and Dee's no-longer-hanging corpse. It wrapped through the door, snaking to a window and back out in order to coil. The slimy appendage next to Dean reeled again.

Dean whined and pleaded.

Melina was dumbfounded.

Ben was curious.

Dee's body flopped sideways. Bits of her flesh clung around the doorframe on the driven spikes. The second appendage stiffened and Dean's branch shook. The looped hold slipped. It recoiled some and the second tail flopped once again. It rose quickly, reaching as it had before. It was twenty feet long, at least. It grasped an overhand framing post and began to roll itself.

"No, God, please no," Dean sobbed.

Melina was agog, but quiet. This was really something unusual.

From the gap beneath, Dean stared down a slimy grey shape. It had yellow eyes with great, solid black pupils. It looked much like a fish but moved like a snake up the banked walls of the deep fissure. It opened its mouth as it reeled itself upward again.

Dean swung his bloody limbs. Useless.

Before Ben fully understood the sum of such a creature, it engulfed Dean to the ankles. It shook and chewed like a pocket dog on a shoe. Dean's cries continued, muffled by the walls of the creature's maw.

"Incredible," Melina whispered.

Ben looked at her and then back at the thing. It was not only stealing kills, but stealing his shine. This was momentous and legendary.

Several wet snaps sounded off and the creature let go of the tree. Dean's legs above the knees remained trapped in Ben's snare. One tail remained topside, but was sliding away, trailing into the fissure.

Ben dragged Melina out and across the lot, palming her scalp. She shuffled and begged, moaning and kicking, trying to relent the pressure atop her head. Once to the edge of the fissure, both looked down into the hole.

Melina gasped and cried out, "No, don't!" Hear eyes begged, like she thought her demise would come from below. Ben was almost offended.

The first tail lashed out again, coiling around a tree. From deep down in the murky green underground, the ugly fishy face began its slow approach. Neither Ben nor Melina noticed the detachment from the overhanging post. The freed appendage tip snaked under Melina and knocked her into the gap as if collecting a loose apple from a tree.

The ground rumbled.

The precarious hold remaining at the roots came away.

Ben watched his final kill fall the distance and splash into the murky waters below. This was not right. This was not fair. This was his deal. He let loose a guttural cry, his masked face pointed toward the moon like a werewolf.

Melina was in that soup, wailing and thrashing, alive. Ben had watched her. She was an excellent swimmer, so maybe…

The appendage that had knocked Melina into the gap coiled around Ben's ankle and he pretended not to notice. Machete at the ready, the slimy tail-like limb tugged and Ben swung with all his fury. Yellowy blood sprayed as if from a fire hose. The injured extremity slipped away, following its brethren.

Down in the mess, Melina dove and then surfaced before swimming from view.

Ben wrapped the machete handle's leather rope around his wrist and began the climb the stark rock slope. He took a long, deep breath. The cavern opened up and he dropped the last thirty-five feet to a stone ledge that sat a meter below the surf. The splash was thick, like landing in paint thinner.

The glow was eerie. The scent was horrid. The air was hot. Giant fish-like creatures swished around him.

Somewhere, not far away, Melina screamed.

—

Ben lifted his gaze after shaking his head to dry the thick fluid from his eyes. The fishy creatures were everywhere, appendages sucked tight to their bodies, tips dangling in the wake of a gentle sway on the glowing green water.

The machete handle met palm and Ben stalked in Melina's direction. She'd pushed her body tight up against a rock wall. Her pajamas clung to her form, her hair dripped down onto her shoulders and chest. One foot had a shoe. One foot was bare. The creature that dragged her down peered at her, toying, swinging its limbs, greenish-yellow fluid trailing and dripping from the wound Ben had delivered. The appendages pressed against the stone walls on either side of Melina and the ugly face lifted and closed distance, as if approaching for a heinous smooch.

Soaked and furious, Ben ran, his feet splashing along the shoreline. Fuck these goddamned fish. He leapt then and slashed the tip of a coiled appendage from another creature on his way by, using its massive body as a stepping-stone from one natural platform to another. It shuddered in pain and swung a good appendage over its back, slapping Ben. He hadn't expected that and stumbled onto the creature's head. He recovered immediately and drove his machete into the thing's great eye. Yellow fluid burst as if from a squeezed grape and then gushed as the body of the thing began to shake. He reared back and slashed long-ways beneath the ruined eye. The creature shook harder. The flow turned greenish.

Up. Ben jumped to the next platform.

The creature playing ultra-bad boyfriend leaned in and opened its mouth. Melina screamed again. The sound echoed as Dean's voice had when the thing had devoured him like he was the meathead version of Jonah.

One-two-three long strides and Ben latched onto a fin. He stabbed nine times. Quaking silently, the creature rocked Ben from its hold. The murky water was hot and Ben fell several feet before charging upward and slashing at the underside of the great green belly. He pushed off and then struggled back to the surface.

No rest to catch his breath. The one he'd injured twice was on him like lightning to a weathervane. It dumped him back under. The moisture dissipated the clay mask, streaky greys and pinks ran rivulets along the surface, dipping in spots around the mesh framework beneath, and clouding before his eyes as he swam. In a blink, the world went dark and he smelled the eggy scent tenfold. The gas was thick and choking him. Sharp walls pressed at him from everywhere above his waist and he understood. The creature had him in its mouth.

He jabbed the machete above his head and the thing coughed him out on a wave of nasty putrid spillage. Up. Up. He reached a platform and scanned the room for his bearings. The thrice-injured thing knew better than to try a fourth round, swimming deep into the endless depths beneath Camp Still Waters.

Ben caught motion across the cavern. Melina was on the move. The wall looked like a huge honeycomb. Melina found a much higher platform that opened into a bright cave.

She obvious sought distance.

Ben sought victim.

The light fell away suddenly and it was darker on the high platform. Through the cave, it grew darker yet. The eggy scent lessened and Ben tried to follow the whimper he assumed belonging to Melina.

They always whimpered.

There were other sounds and then Melina's voice echoed, "No! Ah! *Ah-ah-ah.*"

A huge flare of greenish flame blasted out from a wall, reeking of the eggy gas. Ben lifted his arm to shield his eyes, but saw clearly another wall of options and Melina crawling through a hole. He was about to give chase when another flame burst and he had to wait for the green burn to cease. While he did, he saw Melina's terrified face poke out of the hole a half-second before a green and orange claw pinched over her shoulder and dragged her from sight.

The flame ceased and, nearly blinded by the flash, Ben chased his ears. Melina continued screaming.

He dropped to his knees and blinked, orbs floated over his vision and he bent to peer into the small cave opening. All he saw were shelled legs, like crabs, but standing several feet high. It was brighter in there, but still, his eyes hadn't settled.

No time. He crawled through and began swinging.

Crabs, three of them about the size of a Dodge Neon, each began snapping, trying to catch his machete. They were slow with poor range of vision. The cave had a good many boulders and shadows. A flame burned along the wall where gas trickled like spilled oil.

The one he'd hit with a first, but mostly fruitless swing, led the charge and Ben hopped up on a big rock, avoiding a big pincer. He quickly jumped onto the crab's shell. It squealed a horrid keening sound and another crab moved to strike at him.

Ben had to front roll out of the way as a claw slashed down. Luck was with him. The slash continued until it cracked the shell of the leader and fluid poured like runny egg yolk. The keening grew louder and the third crab charged at Ben on skinny legs.

Too slow this time, Ben wrenched sideways as a pincer came down and tore a hunk from his shoulder. He howled and spun on his ass, kicking out at the skinny legs. The second crab was in it then too and the pair began snapping claws at him as he rolled around the cave.

The machete handle thumped his forearm during a revolution, reminding him of its existence a second before his back connected with a rocky outcropping at the base of the wall. The crabs were feet away and Ben sprang up, dizzy as a drunkard, trying to put the weapon in his grasp as his back pressed against a wall. The machete blade clanked on stone overhead and Ben stumbled again, down onto his ass. His hand finally found handle and he swung back around just as the nearest crab was about to grab on.

The blade was green and on fire.

The strike against the shell did little, but the fire sent both creatures in a backward race. Ben looked at his weapon and then up to the burning wall. He got to his feet and caught his breath, now eyeing the fantastic creatures suddenly cowering from him. The blade went back into the burning fluid and he flicked flames like he was flinging whiffle balls. The crabs skittered, making distance.

Much further down the chamber, a voice cried, "No! No! Nononono!"

Done fucking around with the pair of crabs, he had to save his final girl and restore order to his tableau. He flicked more of the burning fluid at the crabs before taking off after the cries.

—

The crabs had her arms and legs pinched as they carted her in the air along the dim green chamber before clearing another honeycomb wall and stepping into a vast, bright chamber. The walls were wide and fire gullies coursed the floor. The ceiling must've been thirty feet overhead. At the far end, taking up almost an entire wall and reaching two-thirds of the way to the ceiling was a bulbous green shell.

At first, Melina thought it was simply a strange rock. As scared as she was, she clung onto that nothing seemed worse yet, but then stiff eyelids began popping. At first glance, she thought she saw fifteen separate eyes beneath shell outcropping. They blinked often, clicking and chittering. The crabs beneath her began chittering then, too.

Lower, stretching somewhere in the neighborhood of ten feet across and six feet high, another piece of shell slipped upward and a pair of maxillae reached and wiggled like horribly deformed hands.

"No! No! Nononono!" she screamed, trying to free herself from the hold. The crabs held tight and continued on their way, about to serve the enormous terror a meal.

—

Ben Ray Collins felt righteous as he ran into the sea of crustaceans. He dragged his machete into a gulley as he went and flung burning fluid onto crabs. They skittered and parted. At the front of the cave, the only creatures ignoring him had Melina overhead, before tossing her forward, where she landed at the dinner place of the enormous monster.

Ben grunted and sent a goodly sized wave of burning liquid at the foursome standing between him and Melina. They screeched and skittered, crowding at a distance like the other terrified crabs.

The huge thing had Melina in its maxillae and Ben swung down with a deadly rainbow arc, severing one of the appendages. The walls and floor shook.

Ben stumbled sideways, watching as the remaining maxilla dragged Melina into its mouth. Melina gave only a minute amount of struggle, the expression on her face inching toward something like petrified shock.

Ben hadn't come this far to witness the ruination of his life's masterwork by a mindless eating machine. He dove, arms out, into the mouth. Immediately, stinking darkness enveloped him as the machete slipped into meat near the assumed back of throat. A hot gush of fluid washed over him, coming from the wound. Amid the flood and convulsions, he felt around for human body parts. Found a leg and reefed on it.

The cave continued shaking as Ben spun the machete with one hand and dragged at Melina with the other. The hold loosened and she moaned. Ben continued pulling her in reverse and spinning the blade with his other hand. The thing was shaking violently then.

Ben had his hand on the waistband of Melina's pants, was about to let go and reach for steadier, higher purchase, when the thing convulsed an extra-strength effort and a great bathing of half-digested fish-like guts and green stomach water spilled them out of the creature. The wave coursing from the mouth carried them toward the honeycomb wall at the far end of the room. The crabs chittered all over, but were too slow to impede the motion, though a few began giving chase. These ones were caught up in the undertow and reeled in legs to float on the surf.

Melina remained in Ben's precarious grasp, through the first honeycomb wall and stopping against a stone. The caves rocked wildly then and the ceiling began to fall. Ben climbed to his knees, clamped an arm around Melina, and lifted as he stood. The way they'd first come through was sealed off, so he charged into a dark hallway.

He made it thirty blind steps before the ground tipped and his bearing of the floor disappeared. He pitched and lost hold of Melina. The tumble was jarring and short. The chamber remained full dark around them.

A groan sounded to his left and he moved toward it. He swung the machete gently in case something he didn't want to touch had come to visit, but he hit only air.

"Ah!" Melina's screech trailed away in a flash and Ben stood upright and began jogging after the sound. Something had her and was absolutely boogying. The floor began inclining, and Ben had to grab for a wall once he reached the top of a lip that dropped down into another chamber lit by the green streams of gas.

The scene before him was just another impossible situation. Two spiders easily as big as pop-up camping trailers: coarse black hairs jutting from bright green bodies, eyes beyond count, and legs like shiny dogwood branches.

Melina was in an off-white web next to a struggling baby crab. She appeared to be out cold. Ben had to dodge quickly to avoid fired web, and rolled back down the slope he'd just climbed. He paused for a breath, thinking, and then another, it came to him then. He took yet another big breath before charging up the hill and leaping into the open chasm, aiming for nothing, suspecting that he wouldn't land anyway.

He began falling, the ground rising too damned fast. He'd miscalculated the spiders and their shots. He was about to crumble, break his legs at best, break everything else at worst. His hands reached out in the blink and a half it took to fall and they were centimeters from touching before a seeking line shot out and yanked him into a web.

The plan, what little of it that had formed in the back of his mind prior to jumping, was that he'd use the machete to cut himself free from the web after one of the spiders snared him. Trouble was, the only free extremity was his left hand, the empty one. He began struggling against the hold and found it pliable, but unbreakable, something like hot rubber.

He looked across the cavern at the other web. The one spider was busy wrapping the tiny crab while the tiny crab squealed for help or mercy or simply in terror. The other spider danced across the room on nimble legs and made for Ben.

Ben saw his semi-ruined mask in the reflections of those convex eyes grow larger and larger as the thing skittered in tight. It tilted its head back and a slow flow of web began spewing as the front legs collected it, holding it out as if looking to play cat's cradle. It obviously wasn't ready for the punch in the chin. The webbing dropped onto Ben's left leg and the spider staggered backward, falling to its *eights*.

The eyes fell on Ben again. The spider came forward, head tilting a little less and an acid wash pouring forth. The spray ate through the shoulder of the stolen prison guard uniform. Ben groaned at the pain and forced his arm into the spray to grab at the spider's eyes. Fingers closed against the hard balls and the spray ceased. The spider tried to reel away, kicking its forelegs frantically at Ben's arm while backpedaling with the other six.

Ben growled like a beast and one of the eyes popped beneath his grasp and his middle and ring fingers dipped into a socket, twisting the sinews beneath the surface. The spider ceased kicking with its forelegs then and attempted to yank away from the hold. Ben didn't give an inch, but the cords trailing into the spider's skull began to. The further it pulled, the more interior material and eyeball gunk remained in Ben's grasp. Frantic, the thing charged forward, spewing an un-aimed spray of acid onto the web, freeing Ben's left leg. Sensing increased range, he stomped sideways against one of the middle legs. It snapped and the thing teetered, the acid spray cutting a painful line an inch above Ben's bellybutton, trailing right to left.

Ben screamed a guttural bout of nonsense before twisting his hand and slamming his foot into the spider's suddenly available abdomen. He kicked four times beyond the final flinch of the creature to be sure it was dead. He lifted his foot, pulling the spider upward, so he could adjust his hold. Hand on the spider like it was a puppet, he trailed the mouth over the webbing holding his arm. Once his right arm was free, he dragged the spider's face down his side, shaking it now and then to try for more acid. Eventually, he gave up and began cutting with the machete.

Once down, he looked over to the other web. The spider was up in a corner, watching a shadowy hallway. Ben let his eyes fall to the crab and then...

Where had she gone?

Where was the woman?

"What? What?" Melina's voice trailed from the cave mouth. "What the hell…?"

This was something new and different. This had a plea aching for understanding. Ben stood on shaky legs and did his best to hurry to the opening in the rock. There was light in the distance and figures passed before it, shadowy, mysterious silhouettes. Ben looked back to the spider and then to the whining baby crab. He considered putting the crab out of its misery, but changed his mind—didn't like things fucking with his kills either.

—

The lighted space slowed Ben further. The flames were gone, but the shine remained. Greenish-yellow slime covered the walls and glowed like radioactive ooze. And for all he knew, that's what it was. He avoided touching and peered onto big, furry figures. They were muscular and Albino pale. They had great white mops of hair atop their heads and ghoulish pig-like faces.

His first thought was, *Morlocks.* His second was, *Sasquatches.*

They're real.

Right or wrong on either account didn't matter. The beasts had his final girl and that wasn't right. Ben's mouth moved as if speaking. Only a low choking noise emitted from his bloody, clay-smattered lips. He wanted to tell these nearly human freaks that they had something of his and if they wanted to live…but really, they were bigger than he was, and there were a gang of them.

He growled again and trailed the movement, plotting.

The things dragged Melina through another opening. The

floor ascended on a gentle slope. Ben took his time. He had to be more careful with anything even slightly humanoid, not to mention something thinking and large. Bigger brains, bigger trouble.

And there were a ton of them. *How and why had they hid down here?*

Ben shook off the thought, he wasn't supposed to think, he was supposed to act. That was the part that chose him. His resurrection wielded the blunt force energy of a hammer, not the maniacal menace of a scientist.

His hand came up and he touched the mask.

Yes.

Through a winding corridor, onto a slim hallway, they drove deeper into the earth. Another quake shook and Ben bounced against a gooey wall—it was warm. He leaned until the motion ceased. Ahead, Melina screeched anew. This time it was fully terrified—there was no more hope to discuss things with the freaks.

Ben was out of time to assess and address with a clear series of steps.

The world continued to shake and Ben ran as hard he could while maintaining equilibrium.

—

Looming high were steel barrels, pieces of a railway car, and collected, but spilled, runoff from metals used in mining and extraction. There was a steel sign flipped sideways and made porous by the harsh fluids trailing over it. The reasons were all there, Dee's little lesson about politics and the environment. The barrels featured the words *Methane Pioneer*. The sign beheld the initials ACC, in small script below, *Aluminum Company of Canada.*

She came to a stop in the many hands of the freakish beasts. They breathed hot, fishy garbage and slobbered yellowy-green tendrils from the corners of their droopy mouths. She screamed again, sure she knew what was coming.

The waste pile was their god and they'd brought Melina forth for sacrifice. Around her, many of the creatures began humping each other. Many had multiple organs, mostly hidden but there nonetheless. Furry penises went into furry vaginas and anuses. Furry vaginas scissor-ed against other furry vaginas, and against anuses. Those holding Melina heralded dog-like rockets poking out from the white fur. Others yet rubbed their double slits with free hands—*paws?*

Horror reined and Melina had never been less interested in anthropology.

The earth quaked anew and the monument before her shifted and burbled horrid carcinogenic liquids. Two of the horny freaks broke forward and lapped in the fluid. It burned flesh and coat like acid and they squealed in delight even as their fur sloughed away and their skin blistered, burst, flaked, and peeled in great swatches.

Feet pounded the backs of Melina's knees and she fell to a kneel. Hands forced her forward and down. The scent from six inches away burned deep into her sinus. Tears burst and she whined, wishing for a god, any god, to intervene, even praying that Neil deGrasse Tyson or any lingering atoms of Carl Sagan might appear like Superman to rescue her.

The six-inch gap disappeared and the fluid seared her cheek

like a cattle brand, kissing with a pain she'd never known before.

———

Fury reigned. Ben saw *his* girl, one of *his* kills, the final of a master list, on the verge being effectively stolen from him. He charged, swinging. The insatiable beasts stood zero chance while in the passions of coitus.

Ben felt righteous again. He had wounds and pain, but this was where he belonged. This was destiny.

Blood showered and spat. He hacked and kicked. Beasts wailed moments too late to save themselves. He'd killed dozens of people and things before, but none mattered as much as this route. This test was big and he'd waited years in a cell to take it.

The machete slammed into necks and shoulders. More blood spilled, pale pink like cartoon flamingos ground into milk. Heads turned in unison. Great mouths cried out. There were only five separating Ben from Melina. Bony fingers dug and gouged at him from behind. Ben's swings shortened and caused less damage. The underground creatures didn't crumble like humans. They were stronger, more resilient.

———

Melina understood the departing weight from behind and shot up. *Away* from the nasty burning chemical waste was the only thought in her addled and bubbling head.

The room was long and ten yards from the molten idol was another hallway. It was dim beyond and coursed on a decline. It wasn't up, the direction to the surface, but it was away. Good enough. Melina chased distance from the painful demise threatening her and the freaks who'd suddenly, inexplicably, let her go.

—

The beasts had Ben down to a knee. Seeing Melina break from sight brought home a biological strength akin to Popeye's spinach. Thrashing and kicking, the nasty beings toppled sideways, some took a breath to cradle injuries. More beasts pounced, bleeding and wailing. Ben let his machete dangle from his wrist and tossed one and then a second onto the chemical waste. He witnessed Melina's route better then and knew how he'd get a chance to track her down yet.

Suddenly, it was almost as if they wanted to burn. The beasts ran into his arms steadily like children at the gateway of a bounce castle, and he hip-tossed them one by one. It was a solid wall beneath the weeping fluids and the beasts hopped and splashed, and writhed in pain, bits of flesh sloughing away, tufts of hair melting in a sizzle. Eyes popped and that pink blood boiled.

But they wanted it and Ben would oblige until they let him stop.

He threw six more before they began leaping into the waste on their own, burning for their god. Free to do so, Ben chased the route Melina took. The moan and wail of the otherwise quieted freaks behind him dulled further as he charged down the hall. Ahead, Melina grunted and whined. Ben caught up in only twenty barrelling steps.

Melina screamed anew as his hands landed on her shoulders. He swung the machete over her head. He had her, but the setting wasn't correct. The machete connected with steel.

A door was before them, as if someone had been down there before, as if some machine had been there all along. Something like a submarine, but different, more like...*aliens?*

Ben wondered this for two heartbeats as he swung again and then yanked on the rusty handle of the hatch door. He grunted. Melina was still trying to pull away, but he ground fingers into her armpit. With his other hand, he spun the wheel.

Behind him, the beastly cries drew closer and he cast a look back. They looked like wax figure left out on a Texas sidewalk in the middle of August. They moved like a wave directly behind them. Fast, too fast. Ben yanked and spun the hatch handle more. Destroyed beastly skin touched skin. Ben grunted and reefed as the beasts tried to pull him and Melina back. The hatch door opened and lake water burst forth.

The rush sent the beasts away, barrelling down the hallway in reverse, toward the opening. The rush did not slow and Ben used Melina as a shield and pushed up into the relatively clean lake water bounding over them.

It was hot.

The push was incredible, his feet slipped and the pressure suddenly in his ears made it seem as if his head was on the verge of exploding. He pulled his body against the flow and slipped sideways, the tow dragging him, but not even half as strong as the pressure he'd passed through.

———

The water pounded into Melina faster than she expelled it. Hacking and gagging, she finally turned her head enough to breathe one sip of putrid eggy air before the water engulfed her completely. It hurt like crazy, all over it hurt, but the pressure holding her was gone and she needed to swim, up was a notion her body understood and she swam on instinct, there was a pinprick of light somewhere up there, it was far, she had to close her eyes to the heat of the liquid, feeling something like squeezed grapes, her bulbs swelled and throbbed.

She could make if she just…an eel with a mouth like a snake and the skin of a gator glowed pale green before her. She opened her mouth, expelling what remained of her banked oxygen. The creature opened its mouth to attack.

—

The little of mask remaining on Ben's face, though mostly clay sludge, still held off some of the pressure pounding into him as he quickly acclimated to the deep water beyond the hatch. He swam behind Melina. She began to thrash. Not two seconds passed and he came to understand why. Another of the Goddamned creatures was trying to steal what was his.

The thing had no time to react. Ben flung his arm, sending the handle of the machete into his grasp and then slicing the serpentine thing down the center of its face like a split wishbone. Vibrant green blood burst in a Rorschach cloud. The creature began falling and was almost immediately out of sight.

Ben grabbed Melina with his left hand and swung with his right—machete still in grasp in case something else needed killed. His feet kicking continually.

The pinprick was suddenly before him—not so far, making it much too small. He punched and pounded and slashed at the crumbling stone. Pain shot up his arms and throbbed at his wrists. Another quake shook. Ten feet to his left, a gentle lessening of darkness revealed a promising route and he swung Melina upward. She no longer kicked or struggled at all.

His lungs burned for breath as he released the last of his held oxygen. Up. Up. The moon was there. So were more of the giant fish creatures. Ben ignored them and kicked while he had the power to do so.

15

Melina awoke on a cot. Her chest ached incredibly. Her face had smeared and dried blood all over. The spot where she had the chemical burn was hot bubbles beneath her fingertips. The air in the bunkhouse reeked of the eggy scent. But her clothes were dry.

She gasped, recalling her last awake moments under the lake.

Everyone else was dead and there was a mutated underworld directly beneath the lake…and there was a serial killer.

She touched her face again and a bubble popped. It was damp and warm. Pus oozed onto her fingertips. She shook and cried. The danger was not over. That freak in the hockey mask rescued her for something and if she could get away without knowing why, that's what she'd like to do. On shaky legs, she stalked to the window. Enormous dead creatures floated upside down in the lake, as if boiled noodles instead of terrifying abominations. There was a stack of the freakish underground beasts and crabs and something beyond her comprehension.

Birds—natural looking, *thank God!*—pecked at the buffet of dead things.

The man in the mask was nowhere in sight.

"Okay. Okay. Good," she whispered and turned to find clothes and a way out of there. Melina's legs became jelly. "No, please."

———

Ben loomed, coated in green and pink, lifeblood withdrawn at violent ends. The Jacques Plante mask had deteriorated to wire and goo while he'd performed CPR on Melina. It was a lovely surprise when she hacked up water, but a real letdown when she didn't wake up right away. Still, it gave him time to visit Starlita's Delica and select a new mask. Sticking to the crudest, archaic styles, he chose Terry Sawchuck's dogface.

The beasts, those that hadn't drowned, arrived on the surface and Ben toppled them one-by-one while they cowered near the broken-down lodge. The brunt of the fishy creatures started swinging their appendages the following morning, climbing higher and higher until breaching the new surface to touch at the modern world's shores. So while Melina slept, Ben carved the mostly mindless creatures. Only a handful of crabs made it topside and Ben used a mini-sledgehammer on their shells before slashing into their meat.

Once he'd conquered what he saw, he waited at Melina's side for thirty more hours before she finally shifted and he backed into the shadows. Seeing her rise gave melody to his purpose. This was destiny.

She whispered to herself and then barked at him.

It didn't matter.

"No! Please!" she screeched again.

Ben grabbed her by the hair, kneed her in the vagina so her hands were out of the way, and swung a swooping, hooking arc.

The machete made clean work and he held a perfectly severed head.

Glorious.

———

In the UBC company research vehicle, box of replica goalie masks on the seat next to him, Ben rolled slowly, knowing that once the feel of the wheel came back, he'd be good as gold to drive forever. His count was an endless task, entwining the destinies of so many.

He thought maybe next time he'd use a Gerry Cheever mask, ticking off lives until this particular period ended. But the dogface had some use yet too. There were so many faces in that box. So many paths to hall of fame status.

THE END

CHECK OUT OTHER GREAT HORROR NOVELS

DEATH CRAWLERS
by Gerry Griffiths

Worldwide, there are thought to be 8,000 species of centipede, of which, only 3,000 have been scientifically recorded. The venom of Scolopendra gigantea—the largest of the arthropod genus found in the Amazon rainforest—is so potent that it is fatal to small animals and toxic to humans. But when a cargo plane departs the Amazon region and crashes inside a national park in the United States, much larger and deadlier creatures escape the wreckage to roam wild, reproducing at an astounding rate. Entomologist, Frank Travis solicits small town sheriff Wanda Rafferty's help and together they investigate the crash site. But as a rash of gruesome deaths befalls the townsfolk of Prospect, Frank and Wanda will soon discover how vicious and cunning these new breed of predators can be. Meanwhile, Jake and Nora Carver, and another backpacking couple, are venturing up into the mountainous terrain of the park. If only they knew their fun-filled weekend is about to become a living nightmare.

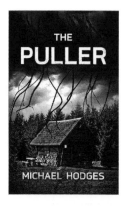

THE PULLER
by Michael Hodges

Matt Kearns has two choices: fight or hide. The creature in the orchard took the rest. Three days ago, he arrived at his favorite place in the world, a remote shack in Michigan's Upper Peninsula. The plan was to mourn his father's death and figure out his life. Now he's fighting for it. An invisible creature has him trapped. Every time Matt tries to flee, he's dragged backwards by an unseen force. Alone and with no hope of rescue, Matt must escape the Puller's reach. But how do you free yourself from something you cannot see?

SEVERED**PRESS**

facebook.com/severedpress

 twitter.com/severedpress

CHECK OUT OTHER GREAT HORROR NOVELS

BLACK FRIDAY
by Michael Hodges

Jared the kleptomaniac, Chike the unemployed IT guy, Patricia the shopaholic, and Jeff the meth dealer are trapped inside a Chicago supermall on Black Friday. Bridgefield Mall empties during a fire alarm, and most of the shoppers drive off into a strange mist surrounding the mall parking lot. They never return. Chike and his group try calling friends and family, but their smart phones won't work, not even Twitter. As the mist creeps closer, the mall lights flicker and surge. Bulbs shatter and spray glass into the air. Unsettling noises are heard from within the mist, as the meth dealer becomes unhinged and hunts the group within the mall. Cornered by the mist, and hunted from within, Chike and the survivors must fight for their lives while solving the mystery of what happened to Bridgefield Mall. Sometimes, a good sale just isn't worth it.

GRIMWEAVE
by Tim Curran

In the deepest, darkest jungles of Indochina, an ancient evil is waiting in a forgotten, primeval valley. It is patient, monstrous, and bloodthirsty. Perfectly adapted to its hot, steaming environment, it strikes silent and stealthy, it chosen prey: human. Now Michael Spiers, a Marine sniper, the only survivor of a previous encounter with the beast, is going after it again. Against his better judgement, he is made part of a Marine Force Recon team that will hunt it down and destroy it.

The hunters are about to become the hunted.

CHECK OUT OTHER GREAT HORROR NOVELS

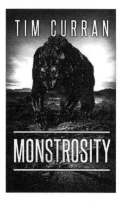

MONSTROSITY
by Tim Curran

The Food. It seeped from the ground, a living, gushing, teratogenic nightmare. It contaminated anything that ate it, causing nature to run wild with horrible mutations, creating massive monstrosities that roam the land destroying towns and cities, feeding on livestock and human beings and one another. Now Frank Bowman, an ordinary farmer with no military skills, must get his children to safety. And that will mean a trip through the contaminated zone of monsters, madmen, and The Food itself. Only a fool would attempt it. Or a man with a mission.

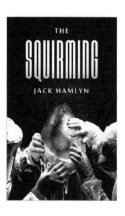

THE SQUIRMING
by Jack Hamlyn

You are their hosts

You are their food.

The parasites came out of nowhere, squirming horrors that enslaved the human race. They turned the population into mindless pack animals, psychotic cannibalistic hordes whose only purpose was to feed them.

Now with the human race teetering at the edge of extinction, extermination teams are fighting back, killing off the parasites and their voracious hosts. Taking them out one by one in violent, bloody encounters.

The future of mankind is at stake.

And time is running out.